About the author

Sir Henry Howarth Bashford was Chief Medical Officer to the Post Office, Medical Adviser to the Treasury and Honorary Physician to King George VI. He published learned medical articles in the *Lancet* and numerous other works of non-fiction including *Wiltshire Harvest, Vagabonds in Perigord* and *The Corner of Harley Street*. This is his only work of humour and was originally published anonymously in 1924.

'Robin', the illustrator, was the *Punch* cartoonist Marjorie Blood. A year after illustrating the book, she took holy orders and became known to generations of girls at Roehampton Convent as Mother Catherine.

Augustus Carp, Esq.
by himself

PRION HUMOUR CLASSICS

* for copyright reasons these titles are not available in the USA or Canada in the Prion edition.

Augustus Carp, Esq. by himself

SIR HENRY HOWARTH BASHFORD

with an introduction by
ROBERT ROBINSON

This edition published in 2000 by
Prion Books Limited, Imperial Works,
Perren Street, London NW5 3ED
www.prionbooks.com

First published in 1924
Copyright © M. Franklin 1924
Introduction copyright © Robert Robinson

A catalogue record for this book is available from the British
Library

ISBN 1-85375-411-0

Jacket design by Jon Gray
Printed and bound in Great Britain
by Creative Print & Design, Wales

Contents

Illustrations

Myself at the age of 21 from a photograph now in the possession of the Reverend Simeon Whey

INTRODUCTION

by ROBERT ROBINSON

When lines from this book float back into my head, I hear my father's voice giving the antiphonal response. I launch into the sermon delivered by the vicar of St James-the Least-of-All, apostrophizing the new lectern (as the narrator himself describes it, 'It gave the general impression of a vulture rather than an eagle...it appeared to have robbed an arsenal of a medium-sized cannon-ball, upon which it now stood poised...'): 'They were all there, [the vicar] trowed, in a double capacity – as human beings, overflowing with gratitude, but also as trustees for the church's furniture. Yes, they were trustees. They must never forget that. That was a distinction that he would have them remember. They were not only human beings, but they were churchmen and trustees – church-beings, trustees and human men,' – and then, echoing across the years, I hear my father chime in, 'Yea, and women also, churchees and trust-men; furniture-women, church-trusts and humanees...'

For this book was part of our private lingo. He'd picked up a first edition from a barrow in Farringdon Road and I didn't just read it, I absorbed it by the special osmosis that in a kindly domestic climate always operates between a parent and a child. There seems never to have been a time when I did not know the family who donated the lectern to which the Carps so violently objected: Alexander Carkeek, a sleeping partner in the firm of Carkeek and Carkeek, fishmongers and poulterers in the Kennington Road ('a northern Caledonian of the most offensive type'), and his two sons, Cosmo and Corkran. (For more than forty years I've never needed to wonder by how slender a margin the brothers avoided actually parting their hair in the middle, and now the original illustrations – by Robin – are restored to a text from which, for me, they were always inseparable.)

Indeed, the characters in the story have always seemed like grotesque relatives I might one day meet: Ezekiel Stool, who had suffered all his life from an inherent dread of shaving, 'the greater portion of [whose] face was in consequence obliterated by a profuse but gentle growth of hair' (holder of high office in the Anti-Dramatic and Saltatory Union, he succumbs to worldliness towards the end; Augustus Carp, once his bosom companion in the distribution of such pamphlets as *Did Wycliffe Waltz?* and *The Chorus Girl's Catastrophe*, runs across him outside Albany. 'Hullo, Carp,' he says, 'Taxi'); and Stool's father, Abraham, proprietor of the famous Adult Gripe Water, who (as Carp records) 'had not then been segregated, but who was already under the impression that he was the Hebrew patriarch, several times insisted upon my approaching him and placing my hand under his left thigh, after which he would offer me, in addition to Mrs Stool, a varying number of rams and goats. Needless to say, I declined to accept these...'

Such minor characters as 'the aunt who stood with my mother's mother at the foot of the stairs' (the admirable illustration, taken 'from a portrait,' conveys the wistful unfulfilment of the permanently overlooked), Mr Beerthorpe the schoolteacher, who is lured away from refereeing a football match so that Carp can present him with a half-pound box of chocolates and tell him what the boys call him ('You are very generally referred to – I trust without foundation – as Beery'), the Rev. Eugene Cake, a low-church evangelist who writes improving fiction – the title of his latest is *Gnashers of Teeth* ('it is even more powerful than *Without are Dogs*'), and Mrs O'Flaherty, the large cleaning-lady who revenged herself on Augustus's father by up-ending him in her pail ('It was a commodious pail, very nearly full with incompletely clean water, and containing in addition the saturate garment with which it was her habit to wash the linoleum. Three separate times she immersed his head in this, even submerging the backs of his ears...') – these comic figures have a curious distinctness reminiscent of Dickens.

Augustus Carp and *The Diary of a Nobody* share common territory. In the *Autobiography of a Really Good Man* we are among the lower-middle-class inheritors of The Laurels, Brickfield Terrace, but now it is the period immediately after the First World War, and Carp's father ('a civic official in a responsible position, being a collector of outstanding accounts for the Consolidated Water Board') is the tenant of Mon Repos, Angela Gardens, Camberwell ('one of some thirty-six admirably conceived houses of a similar and richly ornamented architecture, the front door of each being flanked and surmounted by diamond-shaped panes of blue and vermilion glass; and though it was true that this particular house had been named by the landlord in a foreign tongue, it must not be assumed that this nomenclature in any way met with my father's approval. On the contrary, he had not only protested, but such was his distrust of French morality that he had always insisted, both for himself and others, upon a strictly English pronunciation').

But where the Pooters are kindly and ineffectual, and where even their attempts to patronize the tradesmen (all part of the hierarchy of the parish-pump) make you feel sorry for them, the Carps are hugely unsympathetic, their dignity clamours for sacrifice – even the doctor who fails to cure Augustus's ring-worm is sued before a County Court judge ('evidently addicted to alcohol') – and, in the name of Xtianity (always so spelt), meanness and spite are elevated to operatic levels of booming humbug. It is part of the creative mystery that such a scenario should break the narrow bounds of what might simply have been a lampoon based on a rather snooty view of lower-middle-class bigotry, and become a much less easily defined thing – a sort of fairy-tale.

And here the parallel with an imagination similar to, if less powerful than, that of Dickens suggests itself again. Just as the London from which Mr Pickwick and his friends depart on their adventures is not real, just as that London is a dream, so too is the suburban world of Augustus Carp. There was never a St James-the-Least-of-All (or even a St James-the-Lesser-Still), there was never a father – not even one who was 'the fortunate possessor of an exceptionally large and well-modelled nose' and in whose 'massive ears, with their boldly outstanding rims, resided the rare faculty of independent motion' – there was never a father who wrote inviting the Dean of St Paul's, the Bishop of London, the Archbishop of Canterbury and the Home Secretary to accept the honour of being his son's godfathers. There was never a solicitor like Mr Balfour Whey. His client (Carp senior) having been bruised by the stretcher-bearers who dropped him after the fearful struggle over the lectern ('not only did they drop him in the south transept, but they dropped him a second time in the side aisle, and again upon the threshold of the vestry'), and his wounds obliging him to lie prone upon his mattress, Mr Whey accommodates himself to these exigencies: 'Day after day, even while still lying on his abdomen, [my father] held prolonged interviews with Mr Balfour Whey, who most considerately lay beneath my father's bed, parallel with the sufferer and looking up into his face.' These are oddities, these are monsters, that never were, on land or sea.

They are the more powerful in consequence. Just as no actual person ever spoke like Jeeves or Bertie Wooster or Psmith, so nobody ever spoke like Augustus Carp. Actors impersonating him have been wrong to give him any sort of accent at all; he isn't a cartoon version of a pompous lower-class twit, he is a genie jumping out of some obscure crevice in the imagination of the author – and genies don't have accents. Both Wodehouse and the author of *Augustus Carp* create their own worlds, and those worlds are almost entirely linguistic – Carp is not so much described by the language, as a function of it, he is perceived within the words like a watermark. Language is itself the character.

That is the true mystery, but there are (or there were) attendant mysteries: who was the author, and who was the illustrator? Some twenty years ago I remarked to Anthony Burgess that he appeared to be in the full flower of his southern Metropolitan Xtian manhood and, to my surprise, he recognized the quotation, and proceeded to touch on the questionable morality of descending from an omnibus while the vehicle is still in motion (one of the book's great themes). Prompted by our meeting, Burgess persuaded Heinemann to bring out another edition (it had been first published in 1924) and it was then he discovered the identity of the anonymous author: he was a Dr Bashford, a medical officer in the Post Office, a jolly family man who lived in Hampstead. Later on he was Chief MO at the Post Office and, grander yet, became an Honorary Physician to King George VI. When he died in 1961 at the age of eighty-one (still anonymous, as far as the authorship of *Carp* was concerned), he was Sir Henry Howarth Bashford. But as Pamela Howe, who in 1985 produced a BBC radio programme about the book points out, it was as Dr Bashford of Hampstead, beloved of his wife and family, that he created Augustus Carp.

And who was 'Robin'? The signature had often appeared in *Punch*, but it was not until the radio programme that more was learned: 'Robin' had been Miss Marjorie Blood who, a year or so after illustrating this book, entered the Order of the Sacred Heart and, to generations of girls at the Roehampton Convent, was known as Mother Catherine.

These are the external mysteries, no more than anecdotal, and simply solved. But the central mystery remains, the book itself. Whether we are reflecting upon Augustus's eldritch greed ('Many were the times, for instance, when after a long morning's study, merely interrupted by an occasional cup of cocoa, I turned with avidity to a simple but abundant meal of roast pork and open jam tart, only to find myself, an hour or two later, rolling in agony upon the sofa'), or considering his obsessional attachment to the game of Nuts in May ('My physique stood me in admirable stead in the later stages of the game. For though I was short, with singularly slender arms, my abdomen was large and well covered, while my feet, with their exceptional length and breadth and almost imperceptible arches, enabled me to obtain a tenacious hold of the ground upon which they were set'), at all times, as we read and re-read this bizarre fable, we will find ourselves wondering: from what hidden level, unknown even to himself, was Dr Bashford delivered of a comic masterpiece?

Chapter One

No apology for writing this book. An imperative duty under present conditions. Description of my parents and their personal appearances. Description of Mon Repos, Angela Gardens. Long anxiety prior to my birth. Intense joy when at last this takes place. My father's decision as to my Xtian name. Early selection of my first godfather.

It is customary, I have noticed, in publishing an auto-biography to preface it with some sort of apology. But there are times, and surely the present is one of them, when to do so is manifestly unnecessary. In an age when every standard of decent conduct has either been torn down or is threatened with destruction; when every newspaper is daily reporting scenes of violence, divorce, and arson; when quite young girls smoke cigarettes and even, I am assured, sometimes cigars; when mature women, the mothers of unhappy children, enter the sea in one-piece bathing-costumes; and when married men, the heads of households, prefer the flicker of the cinematograph to the Athanasian Creed – then it is obviously a task, not to be justifiably avoided, to place some higher example before the world.

For some time – I am now forty-seven – I had been feeling this with increasing urgency. And when not only my wife and her four sisters, but the vicar of my parish, the Reverend Simeon Whey, approached me with the same suggestion, I felt that delay would amount to sin.

That sin, by many persons, is now lightly regarded, I am, of course, only too well aware. That its very existence is denied by others is a fact equally familiar to me. But I am not one of them. On every ground I am an unflinching opponent of sin. I have continually rebuked it in others. I have strictly refrained from it in myself. And for that reason alone I have deemed it incumbent upon me to issue this volume.

I propose in the first instance to deal with my earliest surroundings and the influence exerted upon me by my father, believing as I do that every man (and to a lesser extent every woman) is almost entirely the product of his or her personal endeavours. I cannot pretend, of course, to attach much importance to merely paternal influence. Nevertheless in the lives of each one of us it undoubtedly plays a certain part. And although my father had numerous faults, as I afterwards discovered and was able to point out to him, he yet brought to bear on me the full force of a frequently noble character.

That such was his duty I do not of course deny. But duty well done is rare enough to deserve a tribute. And in days such as these, when fatherhood is so lightly regarded, and is so frequently, indeed, accidental, too much attention can surely not be given to so opposite an instance.

At the time of my birth, then, and until his death, my father was a civic official in a responsible position, being a collector of outstanding accounts for the Consolidated Water Board. In addition, he was one of the most respected and trustworthy agents of the Durham and West Hartlepool Fire and Burglary Insurance Company, a sidesman of the Church of St James-the-Less in

Camberwell, and the tenant of Mon Repos, Angela Gardens. This was one of some thirty-six admirably conceived houses of a similar and richly ornamented architecture, the front door of each being flanked and surmounted by diamond-shaped panes of blue and vermilion glass; and though it was true that this particular house had been named by the landlord in a foreign tongue, it must not be assumed that this nomenclature in any way met with my father's approval. On the contrary, he had not only protested, but such was his distrust of French morality that he had always insisted, both for himself and others, upon a strictly English pronunciation.

Somewhat under lower middle height, my father, even as a boy, had been inclined to corpulence, a characteristic, inherited by myself, that he succeeded in retaining to the end of his life. Nor did he ever lose – or not to any marked extent – either the abundant hair that grew upon his scalp, his glossy and luxurious moustache, or his extraordinarily powerful voice. This was a deep bass that in moments of emotion became suddenly converted into a high falsetto, and he never hesitated, in a cause that he deemed righteous, to employ it to its full capacity. Always highly coloured, and the fortunate possessor of an exceptionally large and well-modelled nose, my father's eyes were of a singularly pale, unwinking blue, while in his massive ears, with their boldly outstanding rims, resided the rare faculty of independent motion.

My mother, on the other hand, presented hardly a feature that could, in the strictest sense, have been called beautiful, although she was somewhat taller than my father, with eyes that were similar in their shade of

blue. Like my father's, too, her nose was large, but it had
been built on lines that were altogether weaker, and
the slightly reddish down upon her upper lip might even
by some people have been considered a disfigurement.
She had inherited, however, together with five hundred
pounds, an apparently gentle disposition, and was a
scion or scioness of the Walworth Road branch of
the great family of Robinson. Herself the eldest of the
nine daughters of Mortimer Robinson, a well-known
provision merchant, my father had claimed relationship
for her, albeit unsuccessfully, with Peter Robinson of
Oxford Street, while he used half humorously to assert
her connection with the fictional character known as
Robinson Crusoe. Clean in her habits, quiet about the
house, and invariably obedient to his slightest wish, he
had very seldom indeed, as he often told me, seriously
regretted his choice of a wife.

With sufficient capital, therefore, not only to furnish
his house, but to pay its first year's rent and establish an
emergency fund, my father might well have been
supposed by an ignorant observer to be free from every
anxiety. Such was not the case, however, and he was
obliged, almost immediately, to face one of the sternest
ordeals of his married life. Ardently desiring increase, it
was not for nine and a half months that Providence saw
fit to answer his prayers, and as week succeeded week
and the cradle still remained empty, only his unfaltering
faith saved him from despair. But the hour came at last,
and so vividly has my father described it to me that I
have long since shared its triumphant joy.

Born at half-past three on a February morning, the
world having been decked with a slight snow-fall, it was

then that my mother's aunt, Mrs Emily Smith, opened the bedroom door and emerged on the landing. My father had gone outside to lean over the gate, and was still leaning there when she opened the door, but my mother's mother, with another of my mother's aunts, were standing with bowed heads at the foot of the stairs. Prone in the parlour, and stretched in uneasy attitudes, five of her eight sisters were snatching a troubled sleep, while two fellow-members of my mother's Mothers' Guild were upon their knees in the back kitchen. But for the fact, indeed, that two of my mother's sisters had not, at that time, had their tonsils removed, the whole house would have been wrapped in the profoundest stillness.

My mother's mother was the first to see Mrs Smith, though she only saw her, as it were, through a mist. Mrs Smith was the first to speak, in a voice tremulous with emotion.

'Where's Augustus?' she said. Augustus was my father's name.

'He's just gone outside,' said my mother's mother.

Something splashed heavily on the hall linoleum. It was a drop of moisture from Mrs Smith's forehead.

'Tell him,' she said, 'that he's the father of a son.'

My mother's mother gave a great cry. My father was beside her in a single leap. Always, as I have said, highly coloured, his face at this moment seemed literally on fire. The two fellow-members of my mother's Mothers' Guild, accompanied by my father's five sisters-in-law, rushed into the hall. Mrs Smith leaned over the banisters.

'A boy,' she said. 'It's a boy.'

'A boy?' said my father.

'Yes, a boy,' said Mrs Smith.

There was a moment's hush, and then Nature had its way. My father unashamedly burst into tears. My mother's mother kissed him on the neck just as the two fellow-members burst into a hymn; and a moment later, my mother's five sisters burst simultaneously into the doxology. Then my father recovered himself and held up his hand.

'I shall call him Augustus,' he said, 'after myself.'

'Or tin?' suggested my mother's mother. 'What about calling him tin, after the saint?'

'How do you mean – tin?' said my father.

'Augus-tin,' said Mrs Emily Smith.

But my father shook his head.

'No, it shall be tus,' he said. 'Tus is better than tin.'

Then his five sisters-in-law resumed the singing, from which the two fellow-members had been unable to desist, until my father, who had been rapidly thinking, once again held up his hand.

'And I shall give the vicar,' he said, 'the first opportunity of becoming Augustus's godfather.'

Then he took a deep breath, threw back his shoulders, tilted his chin, and closed his eyes; and with the full vigour of his immense voice, he, too, joined in the doxology.

Chapter Two

Trials of my infancy. Varieties of indigestion. I suffer from a local erythema. Instance of my father's unselfishness. Difficulty in providing a second godfather. Unexpected solution of the problem. The ceremony of my baptism. A narrow escape. Was it culpable carelessness? My father transfers his worship to St James-the-Lesser-Still, Peckham Rye.

With the portion of my life that intervened between my birth and my baptism I do not propose, owing to exigencies of space, to deal in the fullest detail. But it may be of some comfort to weaker fellow-sufferers to be assured that, from the outset, the ill-health to which I have been a life-long martyr played its part in testing my character. Singularly well formed, of a sanguine complexion, and weighing not less than four and three-quarter pounds, Providence saw fit almost immediately to purge me without medicinal aid. Whether this was due, under Higher Supervision, as my father several times forcibly suggested to her, to some dietary excess or indiscretion on the part of my mother was never determined. But the fact remained that for several weeks I suffered from indigestion in two main directions.

Twice, indeed, on the grounds of health, the ceremony of my baptism had to be postponed; and for hours together, I have been told, I lay upon my back, with my knees drawn up and my fingers clenched, in an

7

anguished endeavour to stifle the moans that I was too enfeebled wholly to suppress. Time after time, too, my mother's mother, the aunt that had stood with her at the bottom of the stairs, and various of my mother's sisters would recommend alternative forms of nourishment. But although, at my father's desire, each of these suggestions was given an immediate trial, it was not for two months, and until I had been subjected to a heart-breaking period of starvation, that an affliction abated to which I have since been liable at any moment of undue excitement.

Chastened within, however, as I had been, I was not to escape chastisement without. For no sooner had I begun, in some small measure, to assimilate the food provided for me than I became the victim of an unfortunate skin complaint known, as I am informed, as erythema. This was happily local, but it gave rise to a very profound irritation, and one that proved, as my father has often assured me, to be of a peculiarly obstinate character. Naturally diffident, owing to the site of the affection, to mention it even to the family doctor, my parents exhausted their every resource without procuring the least alleviation. Though for night after night they made it a matter of prayer, my sufferings were pitiful, I have been told, to the last extreme; and almost hourly, from supper-time to breakfast, the darkness was rent with my cries.

Unable at last, owing to his acute sensibilities, to witness my agony any longer, my father was obliged, with the deepest reluctance, to confine himself to a separate bedroom. But it was in this extremity that his almost Quixotic unselfishness shone, if possible, with an added lustre. From the time of his marriage to the day of my birth, and as soon thereafter as the doctor had permitted her to rise, my father had been in the habit of enabling my mother to provide him with an early cup of tea. And this he had done by waking her regularly a few minutes before six o'clock. In view of the fact, however, that he was now occupying a different bedroom, and that, owing to my indisposition, she was awake most of the night, he offered to excuse her should she chance to be asleep at that hour, from the performance of this wifely duty. Needless to say, it was not an offer that she could accept. Indeed, in his heart he had not expected her to do so. And I have even considered the incident, in latter days, as illustrative of a certain weakness in my father's character. But I have never been able to regard it without affection or to forbear mentioning it on appropriate occasions.

That in most respects, however, my father's temperament was an exceptionally unflinching one was amply corroborated by the circumstances attendant upon the choice of my second godfather. This gave rise, as my father has frequently told me, to the most prolonged and anxious discussions, and entailed an enormous amount of correspondence, some of which has been preserved among the family documents. For with his ruthless determination, inherited by myself, to discover and expose every kind of wrong-doing, with his lifelong habit of informing those in authority of any dereliction of duty in themselves and their subordinates, and with the passion for truth that compelled him on every occasion instantly to correct what he deemed the reverse, my father had necessarily

9

but little leisure to cultivate the easy art of friendship. Amongst his acquaintances, indeed, there were but few that even remotely approximated to his standards; and he had found none that his conscience had permitted him to select for the purposes of personal friendship.

It was for this reason that, on the occasion of his marriage, he had dispensed with the services of a best man. And although the vicar had eventually agreed to act as one of my male sponsors, the appointment of a second began to assume the proportions of an almost insoluble problem. It being manifestly impossible to hope for a suitable candidate among such persons as occasionally called at the house, and my father's character having long ago isolated him from his more immediate masculine relatives, he resolved at last to appeal to the public sense of the higher officials of the Church of England.

Nor was the result ungratifying, as various letters still in my possession go to prove. Though unable, owing to so many similar and previously acquired obligations, to accede to my father's suggestion, all of them replied with the greatest courtesy. Thus the Dean of St Paul's wrote in person wishing me every success in life; the Bishop of London trusted that my father's aspirations as to my personal holiness would be realized; while the Archbishop of Canterbury commanded his secretary to express his gratification at the suggestion of an honour that only the exigencies of his position as Primate forbade him to accept. Needless to say, those in charge of the State, whom my father next approached, behaved very differently. Neither the Prime Minister nor the Home Secretary saw fit to reply at all, while the President of the Board of Trade merely expressed a formal regret. And yet in the end, as is so often the case, the solution proved quite a simple one. Turn but a stone, says a poet,* and start a wing. And my father did not even need to turn a stone. Sick at heart, he was returning home one night when he suddenly caught sight of himself in a cheese-monger's window. It was as though Providence, he said, had touched him on the shoulder. Whereas he had been blind, he said, then he saw. For a moment the shock was almost too much for him. A member of the constabulary, indeed, actually asked him to move on. But the solution was there, staring him in the face. Involuntarily he raised his hat. *He himself was the man.*

With my aunt, Mrs Emily Smith, only too eager to be my godmother, everything now seemed to be propitious for the happy consummation of my baptism, and no more earnest or reverent gathering could have been found that day in any Metropolitan church. The vicar being godfather, the actual ceremony was, at my father's suggestion, performed by the senior curate, the junior curate, in deference to my father's position as sidesman, being on the vicar's right hand between him and my mother.

On the senior curate's left stood my father, flanked on his own left by the verger, the circle round the font being completed by Mrs Emily Smith, my mother's mother, my mother's father, her eight sisters and the aunt that had stood with my mother's mother at the foot of the stairs. A soft April rain was refreshing the outside

* I have since learned that he was a Roman Catholic, and I cannot therefore vouch for the accuracy of his statement.

world, and the first part of the service had been successfully performed, when an incident occurred that might well have been attended with the most tragic and irreparable consequences. For there suddenly took place, just as I had been handed to the senior curate, so acute an exacerbation of the erythema that, in the ensuing convulsion, he was quite unable to retain me in his grasp.

I say unable, but, as my father pointed out to him immediately after the close of the service, had I suffered any provable damage he would certainly have taken legal advice. Falling from his arms, however, I remained poised for a moment upon the extreme brim of the font, and then fell forward, colliding with the vicar, who stumbled backwards in his efforts to save me. From the tottering vicar I then ricochetted, in what I believe is a military phrase, towards the feet of the junior curate, who became unexpectedly the instrument of Providence. I do not myself practise, nor do I greatly approve, any form of purely athletic exercise. But it was perhaps fortunate that the curate in question happened to be a skilful player of cricket. For just as my head was within an inch of the floor and the blood had receded from every countenance, he shot out his hand and succeeded in catching me in a position technically known, I believe, as the slips.

'Oh, well held, sir!' cried the senior curate, and then for a moment or two his emotion overcame him.

The vicar, still pale, recovered his balance.

'Poor little Augustus,' said my mother; 'it's the irritation.'

My father frowned at her.

'Without prejudice,' he said. And then for perhaps half a minute there was a deathly silence. It was fractured, I have been told, by myself, as the junior curate handed me back to the senior.

But my father intervened.

'Not again,' he said. 'Never again; never in this world.'

The silence was resumed, broken only by myself. My father stood holding me, trembling with emotion. The vicar took a deep breath.

'Is the service to proceed?' he asked.

'Certainly,' said my father. 'But in other hands.'

It was another instance of his dominating character, but also of his innate sense of justice.

'I am not insensible,' he said to the senior curate, 'of the services that you have already rendered. But in the interests of my son, as you must surely agree, I cannot again trust him to your care.'

The senior curate bowed, but did not articulate a reply, and my father then handed me once more to the junior. For a moment the latter hesitated, but at the vicar's request accepted the privilege of concluding my baptism. Later, I have been told, there was a certain amount of argument, in which my father more than held his own, finally absolving the vicar from further sponsorial duties and notifying his decision to transfer his worship elsewhere.

For a man of my father's position this was a serious step. But it was one that he did not hesitate to take. And within a year, as I have always been proud to remember, he had made himself a sidesman at St James-the-Lesser-Still, Peckham Rye.

13

Chapter Three

Apart from the ill-health to which I have previously
made reference, but which was punctuated with
intervals of comparative well-being, I have always
regarded my first five or six years as a particularly
fruitful period. At my father's desire, almost in this case
a command, my mother began to study various books
on childhood, such as Dr Brewinson's *Childish
Complaints*, Mrs Edward Podmere's *Diet in Infancy*, the
Reverend Ambrose Walker's *First Steps in Religion*,
Wilbur P. Nathan's *The Babe and the Infinite*, Mrs
Wood-Mortimer's *Clothes and the Young*, and Jonathan
and Cornwall's *Dictionary of Home Medicine*. Each of
these, with the exception of the *Dictionary*, was
borrowed in turn from the nearest public library; and it
became my mother's custom to consecrate her afternoon rest hour to the perusal of these volumes.

According to an arrangement suggested by my
father, she would study one chapter each afternoon, or

alternatively three and a half pages of the *Dictionary of Home Medicine*. On his return from work, and after she had washed up the supper dishes – for my father at this time did not employ a domestic – he would put her through a searching examination upon what she had read earlier in the day. If, as was frequently the case, since my mother was not naturally scholastic, she failed to satisfy her examiner, he would playfully impose upon her the little penalty of again going through her task before she went to bed. And on such occasions, if he had not fallen asleep, he would re-examine her when she came to bid him good-night. If, on the other hand, her replies had been judged adequate, it was an understood thing that she might claim an extra kiss. So seriously, indeed, did my mother apply herself that she began to grow unattractively thin; and once, when she had failed in her examination on three successive nights, she actually burst into tears. For this feminine weakness, when she asked his pardon, my father, of course, readily forgave her, merely pointing out that, with my future at stake, he was obviously unable to relax his standards.

Regarding me thus, from the very first, as a sacred trust committed to their charge, this is but a small example of the immense and unremitting care with which my parents undertook me. But it will at least suffice to show that they had not underrated the high task for which they had been called. To my father especially, as the months slipped all too quickly by, I became inexpressibly dear; and it was for that reason, among others, that I escaped the torments of vaccination. Though Jonathan and Cornwall's *Dictionary of Home Medicine* advocated this operation on historical grounds, my father had an instinctive, but none the less well-reasoned, horror of the knife. Himself the subject of frequent boils, he would never permit these to be lanced, invariably giving orders that they should be poulticed until Nature herself brought about their evacuation. Nor can I say that, in my own case, he has been other than completely justified. It is true that I have suffered, and still do suffer, apart from the indigestion previously referred to, from several forms of neurasthenia, a marked tendency to eczema, occipital headaches, sour eructations, and flatulent distension of the abdomen. But from smallpox, although entirely unvaccinated, I have always remained singularly immune.

A similar prescience, too, sufficed to protect me from the anguish and indignity of personal chastisement. For although in principle my father was an ardent supporter of this, and indeed had administered it to several of his relatives' children, he had never required it, he said, in his own case, and did not propose to have it inflicted on me. And it was the abrogation of this rule, although not until my seventh year, by the son of a powerful Hibernian charwoman that first revealed to me, in a never-to-be-forgotten flash, some of the profoundest depths of human iniquity.

It was soon after my sixth birthday that my father was first compelled to employ a charwoman, owing to an attack of unconsciousness on the part of my mother. For several months she had been complaining of breathlessness, incident upon certain of her domestic duties, such as floor-scrubbing, home laundry-work, cleaning the front steps, and polishing the boots and shoes. With his usual consideration my father had instantly remitted various other tasks proper to her position, such as the baking of bread twice a week, and the knitting of the family socks and stockings; and he had further excused her from my own daily tuition in both Latin and arithmetic. Involving, as these subjects did, considerable previous preparation, this was, of course, a sensible relief, obtained though it was at some hazard to my own intellectual future. But despite all these concessions, she continued to be unwell, and finally, as I have said, lapsed into unconsciousness.

For a brief period, therefore, and after medical advice, my father resolved to employ extraneous aid, and at a very considerable financial sacrifice engaged a person called Mrs O'Flaherty. The widow of a colour-sergeant, and one of the church scrubbers, she was highly recommended by the vicar of St James-the-Lesser-Still, and was not devoid, in certain deceptive respects, of the superficial charm of her race. Ominously developed as she was, both below and above the waist, her features were informed with an unintelligent but specious cheerfulness; and these, together with a not unattractive complexion, sufficed for some time to impose upon my mother.

My father, from the beginning, had his doubts of her character, but in view of the vicar's recommendation, decided to employ her; and for the first month or two, apart from her habit of singing, found no cause for particular complaint. He even went as far, upon my mother's intercession, as to allow the woman to bring her youngest child with her, a somewhat gross and over-

18

exuberant lad a few months younger than myself.

That this youth, practically a gutter-snipe, and afterwards a private in the army, should have become a Brigadier-General in the late war, and even have received, as I understand, some kind of decoration, was one of the most deplorable of the many social upheavals for which that disaster was responsible.

From the very outset, with that sensitiveness of vision granted by Providence to certain children, I regarded this new intruder with the deepest suspicion. Obviously inheriting the physique of his mother, and as it seemed the proclivities of his father, his chief article of amusement appeared to be a small cannon, equipped with a spring for purposes of propulsion. This he offered to lend me on the occasion of his first visit, but declining his advances I moved to another room, where I continued my study of a book upon the apostles, written for the young by a Somersetshire clergyman.

Undeterred, however, by a reticence that should have been more than sufficient for a boy with the least good feeling, Desmond, for that was his pretentious name, made a similar offer on his second visit. Again I declined and removed myself, subsequently mentioning the matter to my father, who instantly gave orders that for the future Mrs O'Flaherty's boy was to be confined to the kitchen.

'You will kindly make it clear,' he said, 'to your son that I cannot have my own son disturbed, and that admission to my house does not necessarily include admission to my social circle.'

Unfortunately, owing to a very natural slip due to the rapidity of his elocution, my father pronounced these words as sershle soakle; and I have never forgotten the vulgar and ill-concealed grin with which Mrs O'Flaherty promised to attend to the matter.

Upon the following Saturday, however, a beautiful day in June, with the gerania in the front garden in full bloom, Desmond O'Flaherty again began to make overtures to me through the open door of the kitchen. The parlour door being again ajar, I was, of course, visible to him as I reclined on the sofa; and I instantly observed that he had brought his cannon with him and that its muzzle was pointing towards myself. Informing me that his pocket was full of peas, suitably dried for the purposes of ammunition, he then invited me to become his companion in a game of definitely military character.

This I refused, and I can still recall every detail of all that followed. Happily employed combing a grey rabbit, to which I was deeply attached, and which I had named, but a day or two previously, after the major prophet Isaiah, I heard a faint click, and the next moment was violently struck upon the back of my hand. Unable to suppress a cry of pain, I involuntarily tightened my grip on Isaiah, who suddenly turned his head and made a movement as if about to bite my index finger. Realizing as I did, from my knowledge of the *Dictionary of Home Medicine*, the fatal consequences that might possibly have ensued, I flung him from me and sprang to the floor, almost beside myself with fear and anguish. With an expression of reproach that cut me to the very heart Isaiah then retreated behind the harmonium; and at the same moment I heard a raucous laugh proceeding from the direction of Desmond.

But for Desmond and his mother I was alone in the house, yet I did not hesitate to advance towards the kitchen and grind the cannon beneath my foot. Twice I stamped upon it in what still seems to me a wholly righteous indignation, and in a couple of seconds I had reduced it to an irreparable wreck. For a moment Desmond said nothing. I had taken him by surprise. But then he rushed towards me with a kind of snort, and fiercely hit me on a face already suffused with tears. I turned away from him shaken with sobs. But his bestial appetites were still unsated. A second and a third time he hit me, on both occasions on the neck, and followed this up by an assault with his foot upon the lower portion of my back. But my cries, now almost amounting to shrieks, had by this time attracted Mrs O'Flaherty, and at the same instant my father, returning early, unlocked the front door. In a flash I was in his arms and had sobbed out to him the whole pitiful tale. I felt him quiver and then control himself, as he gently placed me to one side. Then he advanced to Desmond, pointing to the crumpled cannon.

'Pick that up,' he said, 'and leave this house for ever.'

Desmond replied insolently that he would not do so, whereupon my father struck him smartly upon the cheek. For a moment Desmond glared at him, and then, lowering his head, he rushed at my father, beating him with both fists. Taken unawares, my father was obliged to sit heavily down upon an entirely unpadded hall chair, and once again I observed a malignant smile upon the face of Mrs O'Flaherty. But it was only momentary. For, thrusting the little savage away from him, my father hit him twice with the handle of his walking-stick.

As well aimed as they were richly deserved, these blows took instant effect, the first knocking the evil lad sideways, and the second dividing the integument of his forehead. Suffering though he was, my father then rose to his feet and was once more about to address Desmond, when Mrs O'Flaherty, revealed in her true character, ferociously caught him by the shoulders. As I have already recorded, she was a woman of repulsively over-developed physique, and she now began to shake my father so violently that his upper denture fell to the ground.

'You little whelp!' she cried, with incredible blasphemy, 'you little whelp of a bullying puffball!'

Then to my horror, no less than to his own, she lifted him bodily from the ground. For a brief moment, or so it seemed to me, I was on the verge of a merciful oblivion, but the next instant I beheld Mrs O'Flaherty thrusting my father's head into her pail. It was a commodious pail, very nearly full with incompletely clean water, and containing in addition the saturate garment with which it was her habit to wash the linoleum. Three separate times she immersed his head in this, even submerging the backs of his ears, and when at last she released him, and he had regained his breath, he was more moved than I had ever seen him.

Always eloquent, his denunciation of her conduct, deservedly attuned to the level of her understanding, was of a severity that has scarcely been equalled even in the writings of my rabbit's namesake. Time after time, with a holy passion that repeatedly interfered with his respiration, he felt it obligatory to adjure his Creator to consign such a soul to its just perdition. And when Mrs

O'Flaherty handed him his upper denture he dashed it once more to the ground. Finally he commanded her to leave the house instantly, frankly informing her that he should prosecute her for assault.

'Yes, it'll look real nice,' she said, 'in the local papers, chippin' a child's 'ead open and 'avin' yer own in a pail.'

The malevolence with which she said this was almost inconceivable. But, as my father pointed out to me when she had gone, it raised issues of the profoundest importance that would demand his most serious consideration. For while in his own person — *in propria persona* * – it might be his duty to bring her before the magistrates, it might be no less important, as a sidesman of the Established Church, to avoid the contingent publicity. This, indeed, was the decision to which he ultimately came, and as an instance of what may be called, perhaps, his sanctified statesmanship, it has always seemed to me to shed a peculiar radiance upon one of the sublimest aspects of his character. With regard, however, to the lethargy, little less than criminal, of the vicar of St James-the-Lesser-Still, I have always been at a loss; and I cannot help suspecting, as indeed my father openly suggested to him, that his relations with Mrs O'Flaherty were not at all what they should have been. For not only did he deprecate, having heard my father's narrative, what he weakly described as any precipitate action, but she was actually observed by an acquaintance of my father's scrubbing the church floor upon the following evening.

Under such circumstances my father had no choice

* In his own person.

but to hasten instantly to the vicarage, where he confronted the vicar with the suggestion – an extremely natural one – already referred to. But his reply, as my father has often assured me, was neither Xtian nor even gentlemanly, and my father was obliged therefore, with the deepest reluctance, once more to transfer his worship. It was a serious step, but he had been fortified with the experience previously forced upon him at St James-the-Less, and in less than five months he had become one of the foremost sidesmen at St James-the-Least-of-All, Kennington Oval.

Chapter Four

Further years of boyhood and additional crosses. Progress in study and music. I excel at the game of Nuts in May. I am to go to Hopkinson House School. But Providence again intervenes. I become a victim of the ring-worm. Devastating effect of an ointment. Mr Balfour Whey and his sons. A brutal County Court judge. But my father obtains damages.

Physically shattered as I had been by the attack on my person by Desmond O'Flaherty, the mental and spiritual consequences of this assault were far more serious and prolonged. Awakened for the first time to the contemporary existence of a depravity hitherto unsuspected by me, I was unable for several weeks to regain my previous composure, or indeed to venture unaccompanied beyond the precincts of the house. Nor could I bear even to contemplate the introduction of a successor to Mrs O'Flaherty.

For that reason, although still in poor health, my mother was obliged to resume her former duties, while my father was confirmed in his decision to postpone my schooldays for another three or four years. To this he had already been inclined, partly owing to the represenstations that I myself had been compelled to make to him, and partly owing to his desire to assist me as far as possible in bearing the crosses with which Providence had entrusted me. Far beyond the average both in weight and number, I can realize now, of course,

what a privilege these were. But in the earlier years of
my boyhood they taxed my faith to its utmost powers.

Many were the times, for instance, when after a long
morning's study, merely interrupted by an occasional
cup of cocoa, I turned with avidity to a simple but
abundant meal of roast pork and open jam tart, only to
find myself, an hour or two later, rolling in agony upon
the sofa, or even indeed summoned on certain
occasions to yield it back whence it came. This was
perhaps the hardest lesson of all. But I am happy to say
that at last I learned it. And I can well remember the
pride with which my father, hurrying into the parlour
with a convenient receptacle, first found me consoling
myself with some appropriate verses from an early
chapter of the Book of Job.

That incident alone, as my father often used to say,
was a complete justification of his decision to postpone
my school life; and I am quite confident that, had I been
earlier subjected to the propinquity of coarser-fibred
boys, I should never have survived to render adult
service to the men and women of my time. Nor should I
have made, I am sure, such intellectual progress as
I achieved between my sixth and eleventh birthdays.
Familiar from cover to cover not only with the Holy
Bible, but also with the Apocrypha, I had attained
dexterity in simple division, was acquainted with the
geography of the British Isles, and had read the history
of England so far as the reign of Queen Anne. Passionately devoted to music, I had taught myself to play
from memory the airs of a large number of well-known
hymns, including several of the more rapid and
accentuated of the late Messrs Moody and Sankey.

Subject to my father's guidance, too, I ranged in boyish fashion amongst literature of a lighter order. With some of the works of Longfellow, for instance, I was soon so familiar as to be able to repeat them without a mistake, and I can still recall the delight with which I read a work of fiction in which Martin Luther was one of the characters portrayed.

Happy as I was, however, with some such volume as this, a pound or two of chocolates, and my rabbit Isaiah, or to settle down for a long summer afternoon with the Hymnal Companion to the Book of Common Prayer, I was not averse from an occasional ramble in the company of my father, or even from exercise of a more vehement order with younger and suitable comrades. The chief of these latter was Emily Smith, the granddaughter of Mrs Emily Smith, my mother's aunt, a gentle child, who was unfortunately an albino, but of a deeply religious and sympathetic nature.

A year or two older than myself, she lived with her grandmother at New Cross, and in her company and that of some of her school companions, I played several health-giving and mirthful games. One of our favourites, I remember, was Hide and Go Seek, combining both physical and mental exertion; and another, of which we were hardly less fond, was known as Nuts in May.

For the purposes of this latter game those who proposed to take part would first form themselves into equal groups, the members of each moiety then standing side by side, facing the same way and holding each other's hands. The two groups would then take up positions, each opposite each, in joyous anticipation, and so arranged as to secure a space between them sufficient for an alternating advance and retreat. By a previous arrangement one of the two sides would then approximate itself to the other, singing in unison and to an established melody, the following humorously incongruous lines:

> Here we go gathering nuts in May, nuts in May,
>   nuts in May,
> Here we go gathering nuts in May
> On a cold and frosty morning.

That we were not, in fact, doing so was of course obvious. But the innocent laughter that the words always provoked in us was quite sufficient, in the opinion of myself and my comrades, to rob them of any semblance of deliberate untruthfulness.

It would then become the turn of the previously silent and stationary players to advance singing a second stanza, in which they would merrily inquire which of their number was to be chosen as symbolic of these nuts in May. To them in reply the first group would designate a member of the second, whereupon the second group would once more advance with the very pertinent query:

> *Whom will you send to fetch her (or him, if it was myself)*
> *away, fetch her (or him, if it was myself) away, fetch*
> *her (or him, if it was myself) away,*
> *Whom will you send to fetch her (or him, if it was myself)*
> *away,*
> *On a cold and frosty morning?*

The members of the first group would then select one

of their comrades to be the emissary of conveyance, and to the same melody and with a similar gesture, would announce their choice to the second group. A pocket-handkerchief, folded upon itself diagonally, would then be stretched upon the grass, parallel to and midway between the merry and expectant companies of players. The symbolized nut and its would-be gatherer would then face each other across the extended handkerchief, grasp hands, and each earnestly endeavour to draw the other across the separating fabric. To whomsoever was successful the other would then be accorded as a member henceforward of the victor's group, and the game would proceed as before with ever-increasing mirth.

Ultimately it might happen, and indeed it often did, that one of the sides would finally absorb the other, and the absorbing side usually including myself, my services were naturally in the keenest demand. I soon found, in fact, that, in spite of my ill-health, I was singularly adapted to this form of recreation. Inheriting, as I did, to a very great extent, my father's powerful and sonorous voice, I was able to throw myself with dominating effect into the preliminary vocal exchanges, while my physique stood me in admirable stead in the later stages of the game. For though I was short, with singularly slender arms, my abdomen was large and well covered, while my feet, with their exceptional length and breadth and almost imperceptible arches, enabled me to obtain a tenacious hold of the ground upon which they were set.

So proficient, in fact, did I become that when I went to school I was bitterly disappointed to find that this, my favourite game of play, was not even included in the curriculum. In later years I have heard this game criticized both on moral and physical grounds, and even my friend and vicar, the Reverend Simeon Whey, has had grave doubts as to its permissibility. On many occasions indeed we have sat far into the night arguing about its effects on the Xtian character. But I am happy to say that he has now gone so far as to approve of it for others. Indeed, as I have more than once facetiously suggested to him, his real objections to the game have been personal, founded on a lack of success in its practice that may well have prejudiced his outlook. For though he is no mean exponent of the game of Draughts, as well as that of Word Making and Word Taking, at Nuts in May he has seldom, if ever, avoided being drawn across the handkerchief. As the result of my protests, however, he has continued to permit the game to be one of the brightest features of our annual Sunday School gatherings; and most of our school-mistresses, I think, would be compelled to testify that I have retained all my old-time skill.

In such fashion, then, I emerged into my twelfth year; and, albeit with considerable misgivings, my father arranged at last for my entry into a high-class school in the neighbourhood. Known as Hopkinson House School for the Sons of Gentlemen, it was conveniently situated in Jasmine Grove on the southern outskirts of Camberwell, and included features in its dignified exterior of almost every type of architecture. Approached by a semi-circular gravel drive with gates of entry and exit, it was flanked on both sides, and isolated in the rear, by an asphalt recreation-ground.

Above the front steps, two chocolate-coloured pillars supported a classical portico, and the windows of the first-floor rooms were surrounded with characteristic Gothic mouldings. The windows of the first, second and third storeys were of a simpler Georgian pattern, but the roof was uplifted, at its anterior corners, into castellated Norman turrets. Midway between these, an Elizabethan gable formed a pleasing contrast, and the two chimney-stacks, each bearing a lightning-conductor, were decorated with Moorish relief work.

Conducted by a Mr Septimus Lorton, the successor to Mr Hopkinson, the founder of the school, it was daily attended by some seventy or eighty of the sons of the Peckham and Camberwell gentry. Concerning Mr Lorton, I shall have more to say presently; but just about a week before what was to have been my first term, a tender but inscrutable Providence once again intervened. The agent of this new affliction was a parasite commonly known, I understand, as the ring-worm, and within a brief period it had established upon my head no less than four separate colonies. That being the case, not only was my school-life yet a second time postponed, but I was obliged to render up, under medical orders, and that the extent of the malady might be the more easily discernible, the greater proportion of my abundant and not unattractive chestnut hair. To the first of these consequences I was reconciled with no great difficulty, but to the second, I must confess, resignation was not so easy; and for night after night my pillow was moistened with tears scarcely restrained during the day. But worse was to follow. For upon the appearance of a fifth and even more intractable

31

settlement, the doctor in charge of the case took this opportunity of prescribing a wholly unjustifiable ointment. That it slew the parasites was undoubtedly true. But such were the ravages of this violent medicament that, to an accompaniment of the acutest distress, the whole of my hair disappeared.

Even in this, however, probably up till then the darkest hour of my existence, Providence had set a rainbow across my despair from which I have never since failed to glean comfort. Roused to the very depths of his indignant paternity, my father immediately began to take steps against the doctor, while both Mrs Emily Smith, the grandmother of my little comrade, and the aunt that had stood with my mother's mother at the bottom of the stairs, provided me with velveteen skull-caps, skilfully embroidered with forget-me-nots.

Perhaps the most fruitful, however, of the issues of this affliction, apart from the damages that my father ultimately secured, was the lifelong friendship that it produced between ourselves and the Whey family. A junior sidesman to my father at St James-the-Least-of-All, Mr Balfour Whey was not only a rising solicitor, but the father of two boys, Simeon and Silas. To the elder of these, Simeon, I have already referred as the vicar of the parish in which I at present reside. But Silas, since dead under distressing circumstances, to which I shall refer in due course, was but half an hour younger, and they were usually regarded as being twins.

Xtian lads of about my own age, and each with an impediment in his speech, both were destined on this account for eventual ordination in the Church of England. What knitted us together, however, at this

*My dear Father in his prime. taken from a group
of sidesmen of St. James the Less*

painful juncture was the curious fact that, in addition to others, both of them were suffering like myself from an invasion of the ring-worm. Adequately treated however, they had retained their hair, and, as their father immediately perceived, might for this reason prove invaluable witnesses in the prosecution upon which we had determined.

In this Mr Balfour Whey had already consented to act as my father's legal adviser, on the understanding that, if the case should fail, my father should be exempt from the payment of charges, while, if it should succeed, the damages should be shared between them on agreed and equitable terms. An extremely forcible Hibernian barrister was then engaged on a similar basis, and never shall I forget the noble determination of these two earnest and devoted men. Fortified with the assistance, somewhat expensive, but under the circumstances deemed necessary, of an extremely adaptable, intelligent, and experienced medical expert, they proved far too powerful both for the doctor, a young man unrepresented by counsel, and even for the County Court judge, a sinister-looking person, evidently addicted to alcohol. Nevertheless, it was no easy fight and the bias of the judge was obvious from the outset. Time after time when my father rose from his seat in the well of the court to make ejaculations, he commanded him to be silent in a tone of voice that no gentleman should have used to another. And once when my mother's aunt, Mrs Emily Smith, and the aunt that had stood with my mother's mother at the foot of the stairs, rose simultaneously and cried, 'Oh, you story', after an unveracious comment by the doctor, he actually threatened to have them ejected by one of his underlings in the court.

Nor was he more polite to my mother's eight sisters, industrious young women who had brought their knitting, even going so far as to say that, if they continued to rattle their needles, he should have them similarly transported. To this my father very naturally objected in one of his most dignified and impassioned speeches, again cut short, though not without the utmost difficulty, by this self-assertive and presumptuous man. Even to Simeon and Silas Whey, each of whom had covered the Bible with kisses, he behaved in such a fashion as entirely to rob them of their natural joy in being in the witness-box. For though it was true, and only to be expected, that their vocal disabilities were increased by their excitement, he not only professed to consider them irrelevant, but brutally informed them that they were unintelligible. For a moment we were stunned. But then, as one woman, my mother's eight sisters rose to their feet, as did Mrs Balfour Whey, Mrs Emily Smith, and the aunt that had stood with my mother's mother at the foot of the stairs. Led by my father they shouted 'Shame' in tones that shook the very roof, while the Hibernian barrister, with a gesture that I have never seen equalled, swept his papers from the desk before him, and sank speechless into his seat.

It was such a scene as no one in the court had probably ever before witnessed, and even the judge seemed slightly taken aback by the volume of resentment that he had aroused. It was, at any rate, with a distinct tremor and in markedly altered tones that he ordered the proceedings to be resumed. And when I myself, as the prosecution's last witness, proceeded to take the oath in my velveteen skull-cap, his change of colour was so manifest as to become the subject of general comment.

Keeping my face firmly towards him, upon the advice of my counsel, I stood unshaken, albeit not unmoved, during the latter's preliminary remarks. Here was a lad, he said, in the soft and vibrant tones of the convinced and accomplished pleader, the only lad, nay, the only child, the solitary hope of his devoted parents. Too delicate hitherto to have been sent to the school – the scholastic establishment for which his abilities had long since qualified him, he had been happily expecting, with all the ardour that His Honour would observe imprinted on his countenance, to have entered this academy of learning some seven weeks before. But what had happened? His Honour had heard. It was the subject matter of this action. Not only had his career, since time was money, been already seriously crippled, but he had been subjected to a personal mutilation, the moral effect of which it was impossible to appraise. One moment a happy – nay, he might almost say without unduly straining the truth – one moment a happy, but not only a happy, a positively handsome young gentleman, he had been reduced in the next, either by wilful design, by malevolent neglect, or by an infamous want of knowledge, to the spectacle that he would be obliged – how reluctantly His Honour could imagine - to submit to His Honour's inspection.

Here a low ripple of sympathy and horror broke involuntarily from most of those present; and it was perhaps significant, as Mr Whey remarked to my father, that the judge took no steps to suppress it. Then, after a brief question or two, since, as my counsel said, mine was an ordeal that he dared not long prolong, he asked me to remove my velveteen skull-cap and let His Honour see what was underneath. It was an effort. But I achieved it, and the effect on the judge was instantaneous. In spite of his pallor, he had still, up to that point, retained some evidences of his gross habit of life. But now the last vestige of his colour had left him, and he seemed visibly to have lost weight. Contracted to pin-points, his pupils were fixed upon my scalp in a haggard yet fascinated stare; and great beads of perspiration began to glisten upon his forehead. Then, with a sharp expiration like that of a punctured bicycle tyre, he covered his eyes for a moment with his hand, and I knew instinctively, as I replaced my skull-cap, that the case was won.

There were further arguments, of course, and technical exchanges, but to everyone in court they must have seemed of little moment; and I was soon being embraced by father, my aunts and great-aunts, in the happy consciousness that right had triumphed. Nor was that all. For thanks to the damages awarded, my father and myself were enabled to spend a month at Scarborough, while a generous fee was paid by a well-known firm of hair-restorers for a copy of a photograph of my head that my father had thoughtfully taken. Two years later they paid a similar sum for a photograph of the same area normally covered, both being subsequently reproduced, under another name, of course, and with the interval diminished for commercial

37

purposes, as illustrative of the effects of what has since become, I believe, a very profitable commodity.

Chapter Five

First experiences at Hopkinson House School. It is amongst the masters that I hope to find spiritual companionship. I do not do so. Apology of Mr Muglington. I am struck by a football. Subsequent apology of Mr Beerthorpe. Degraded habits of my fellow-scholars. A fearful discovery and its sequel. Amazing ineptitude of Mr Lorton. Concerted assault upon my person. I am rescued by my father, who procures a public apology.

Owing to the successive delays imposed by my general ill-health, the assault upon my person by Desmond O'Flaherty, the sudden invasion of the ring-worm, and the cranial nudity wrought by the ointment, it was not until I was nearly fourteen that I was at last able to attend school; and even then it was perhaps doubtful whether my father should have recommended it. For, although by that time my health was somewhat less precarious, the chastening experiences that I had been called upon to endure had naturally lifted me, in almost every aspect, far above the plane of most of my contemporaries. And while it was true, of course, that in Simeon and Silas Whey I should find sympathetic and well-liked comrades, I was so much older, both mentally and spiritually, than such of their acquaintances as I had chanced to meet that it was only amongst the masters that there seemed any reasonable hope of obtaining an equal and appropriate companionship.

It was to this end, therefore, while endeavouring at the same time to place my services at the disposal of my fellow-scholars, that I resolved from the outset to encourage my tutors to perceive in me a staunch and valuable associate. For the first few days this was not of course easy, owing to the natural confusion incident upon a new term, and it was only by the interjection of an occasional informative remark that I was enabled to adumbrate my ultimate purpose.

Thus when our form-master, a Mr Muglington, asked me if I knew the capital of Belgium, I replied that while I had not as yet enjoyed the opportunity of paying the town a personal visit, I had been credibly informed that it was known as Brussels, so indissolubly associated with the well-known brassica.* Though he was a repellent-looking man with a ginger moustache, I had nevertheless accompanied the words with a friendly smile. But he merely stared at me in what I was compelled to recognize as a singularly crude and offensive fashion.

'Let me see,' he said, 'I think your name is Carp.'

'Augustus Carp,' I replied, 'of Angela Gardens.'

'Then kindly remember,' he said, 'to confine yourself in future to the information asked for and nothing else.'

It was, of course, the speech of a peculiarly narrow-minded and vindictive man, fortuitously thrust into a position of authority that had evidently nourished his worst propensities. But I had not as yet realized how deplorably typical he was of the class to which he belonged, and it was a considerable time before I could restrain the sobs that his infamous words had provoked.

* The botanical family that includes the sprout. I am now convinced that Mr Muglington did not know this.

Nor did he fail to take a further and dastardly advantage of my emotion.

'Perhaps,' he observed, with a malignant sneer, 'when you've quite finished chewing the cud, you'd be so kind as to oblige us by enumerating the principal exports of Finland.'

Afterwards, I am glad to say, thanks to the instant and imperative demand of my father, he was obliged to apologize to me both in my father's presence and in that of the headmaster, Mr Septimus Lorton. But it was not an apology, as I discerned at once, founded on any real and heart-felt contrition, and although I assured him that, so far as I was concerned, he might consider the incident closed, it was perfectly apparent to me that I could never in the future admit him to the privileges of friendship.

Nor was I destined to receive a more satisfying response from the next advance that it seemed my duty to make. Excused on moral grounds from the study of French by a special stipulation of my father, I was permitted instead to take extra lessons in German from a Mr Beerthorpe. A stoutly-built man with extremely short sight, corrected by lenses of exceptional thickness, I was at first attracted to this person by an expression of what I soon discovered was a spurious amiability. I was also distressed to find him almost universally alluded to by the first syllable of his name only, to which the letter y, not originally present in it, had been appended by way of suffix.

Whether or not he was aware of this I did not, of course, know, but both as an act of kindness and in justice to myself, I felt it incumbent on me to seek the earliest chance of dissociating myself from such a practice. I accordingly took the opportunity one day, when he was acting as arbitrator in a game of football in the playground, of approaching him and touching him on the elbow and suggesting that I should like to have a few words with him.

'Eh, what?' he said. 'Foul,' and he then blew a blast, I remember, on a small whistle. Taken unawares, I could not refrain from shuddering a little, and instinctively put my hands to my ears.

'Well, what is it?' he asked. 'What's the matter?'

'Perhaps we might withdraw,' I replied, 'to some quieter place.'

'But what's the trouble?' he said. 'Look out,' and he abruptly leapt back to avoid the oncoming football. Not so fortunate, and left entirely unprotected by Mr Beerthorpe's sudden retreat, I received the full impact of the hurtling projectile upon the upper part of my neck and my left ear, and for some moments I was entirely unable to proceed with the conversation. Indeed had the missile been of the egg-shaped variety frequently employed, I understand, in the same barbarous pursuit, the blow might well have had the most serious, if not fatal, consequences. Nor could I help feeling a trifle disheartened to perceive, when I had regained my powers of speech, that Mr Beerthorpe was still callously blowing his whistle in a remote corner of the playground. Under such circumstances many another lad would have been deflected from his purpose. But in spite of what followed, I have always been glad to remember that I did not allow myself to be deterred. Approaching him a second time, I again touched his elbow.

'Good God,' he said, 'are you still there?'

Naturally flinching a little at the expletive, I reminded him that I had still something to communicate.

'Oh, all right,' he said. 'Come along then.'

He handed his instrument to a neighbouring boy.

'Well, what is it?' he asked.

We entered an empty schoolroom.

'Perhaps I may first,' I said, 'ask you to accept this.'

It was a box of chocolates weighing half a pound and tastefully adorned with a lemon-coloured ribbon.

'It is merely a token,' I proceeded, 'albeit I hope an acceptable one, of a desire to inaugurate friendly relations.'

For a moment he stared at it with his mouth open and then made a rasping noise in the back of his throat.

'But look here,' he said, 'you don't mean to tell me that you've interrupted a game of football just to bring me in here and give me half a pound of chocolates?'

'Not wholly,' I said, 'nor even principally, though I am naturally a little wounded by your tone of voice. But I also desired to inform you that you were the subject of a prevalent indignity from which personally I have strongly dissented.'

'Good God!' he said. 'What on earth do you mean?'

After flinching a second time, I lowered my voice a little:

'I thought you ought to know,' I said, 'that you are very generally referred to – I trust without foundation – as Beery.'

For perhaps twelve, or it might have been thirteen, seconds, the silence was only broken by the cries of the footballers. But I observed that his cheeks were suffused with blood and his myopic eyes beginning to bulge. It was a repulsive sight, and then, like Mr Muglington, he stood revealed in his true character. No less intoxicated than the former with the petty authority conferred by his position, his general conduct, as well as his verbiage, was even coarser and more debased.

'Look here,' he said, 'young What's-your-name, I don't know your name, and I don't want to. But if I have any more of your insolence I shall report you to the headmaster. And now you can clear out and take your chocolates with you.'

Stung to the quick, and with the tears running down my cheeks, I nevertheless held up my hand.

'One moment,' I said. 'You have misapprehended me, and it was perhaps foolish of me to have supposed that it could have been otherwise. But I must clearly point out to you, both for my own sake and that of the school to which we both belong, that it will be rather I who shall be obliged to report you for the language that I have listened to this day.'

Florid to an extreme that I have seldom seen equalled, he opened his mouth once or twice in silence. Then he wiped his forehead with the back of his hand.

'I had rather flattered myself,' he said, 'on my temperance.'

'On the contrary,' I said, 'I am obliged to remind you that you have twice openly invoked the Deity.'

'Good God!' he gasped.

I opened the door for him.

'That makes the third time,' I said. 'You will hear

more of this.'

I had preserved my self-control, but it was only with an effort that left me pitiably weak and wretched and induced a gastritis that robbed me of several minutes' sleep as well as of most of my evening meal. Thanks, however, to a second and even more trenchant interview between my father and Mr Lorton, during which it transpired that Mr Beerthorpe was the father of five unfortunate children, he, too, was obliged to apologize to me and give me an undertaking to restrain his blasphemy. But, as my father agreed, it was an apology obviously given with the utmost reluctance and affording no hope of the happier communion to which I had at one time looked forward.

Meanwhile I had not neglected my fellow-students, unattractive to me as most of them were, and more than once had I offered my spiritual services to an inexperienced or erring class-mate. That these had been fruitless I am not prepared to say. But it was perhaps not surprising, considering the standard of the masters, that the general moral status of their pupils should have left almost everything to be desired. Such a rule, for example, as that forbidding the ingestion of sweetmeats during the hours set apart for study was daily infringed, not only by the younger boys, but by many far older than myself. Exhibitions, too, of personal violence were only too common in the playground, and I had even heard boys, presumably the sons of gentlemen, making use of the word damn.*

It was not until nearly half-term, however, under the

---

* I repeat this with regret. But truth is often best served, I have found, by being completely outspoken.

eyes of Mr Lorton, and in the most sacred hour of the scholastic week, that I suddenly became conscious of the existence of an evil that for a moment completely paralysed me. Himself an organizer rather than a scholar, a proprietor rather than a professor, Mr Lorton confined himself, in respect of actual teaching, to the exposition of the Holy Scriptures. For this purpose he visited each class once a week in rotation, the text-book employed being the Lorton Bible for Schools, published by his brother, Mr Chrysostom Lorton. We had been studying, I remember, the Second Book of Kings, and considering the evil reign of Pekahiah, when Mr Lorton suddenly asked the head boy of the form if he could tell him the name of his successor.

This was, of course, Pekah, the son of Remaliah, with whom I had been familiar for several years. But unfortunately my position in the centre of the class forbade my giving an immediate answer. Nevertheless, I perceived, as boy after boy mutely revealed the depths of his ignorance, that I had probably been destined by the grace of Providence to become the means of their enlightenment. What was my horror, then, on this beautiful autumn day, with the November sunlight slanting through the window, to observe Harold Harper, the boy on my left, and Henry Hancock, the boy on my right, each studying the Second Book of Kings under the shelter conferred by his desk. Objectionable lads as I knew them both to be, I had never dreamed them to have been capable of this, and when Henry Hancock rose in his place and without a tremor said, 'Pekah, son of Remaliah,' it was as though each syllable had been a knife deeply plunged into my very vitals. Pale with wrath I rose to my feet.

'Sir,' I cried, 'Henry Hancock was deceiving you. He read his answer from the open Scripture.'

There was a deathly pause.

'And not only that,' I said, 'but Harold Harper was prepared to do the same.'

Mr Lorton removed his eye-glasses.

'Hancock and Harper,' he said, 'stand up.'

They did so, but with marked reluctance.

'Hancock and Harper,' he said, 'is this true?'

They were silent. But their faces betrayed them, as did Harper's Bible, that slipped to the floor.

'Hancock and Harper,' said Mr Lorton, 'I am ashamed of you. You must each write me out fifty lines.'

'But, sir,' I cried, 'in justice to myself, who knew the correct answer without committing sacrilege, nay, in justice to my fellow-scholars, to say nothing of Holy Writ, surely these lads must be subjected to some less trivial and severer penalty.'

Mr Lorton readjusted his glasses. Then he removed them again and began to wipe them.

'Hanper and Harcock,' he said, 'I mean Harcock and Hanper, as Carp has reminded you, you have sinned very grievously. But I hope – er – this publicity, this publicity, I say, will not be lacking in its due effect upon you.'

'But, sir,' I cried, 'these are mere words.'

'They are very serious ones,' he said, 'very serious ones. Also, as I said, you will each write me fifty lines. And now perhaps Smith Major can tell us who Argob was.'

Petrified by the levity with which the very owner of

the school was able to endure so shattering an exposure, I remained standing for several seconds, wholly unable to utter a syllable. And when I sank at last, stunned and unsupported, into the seat from which I had so lately risen, it was as though my boyhood (and indeed this was actually the case) had been finally snatched from me for ever. Nor was this the end. For, when we emerged into the playground, I found myself surrounded by an opprobrious mob, evidently suborned by Harper and Hancock for the purposes of physical assault and battery. Thrust from one to the other, my collar was disarranged, I was several times smitten upon the face, and it was only by the exercise of my utmost lung-power that I succeeded in attracting adult attention. Indeed I am almost certain that I observed Mr Muglington and Mr Beerthorpe lurking supine behind a curtain, and it was by no less a person than my own father that I was ultimately removed from danger.

Collecting an account a couple of streets away, he had instantly recognized my screams, and, abandoning everything, had rushed to my aid just as Mr Lorton hurried into the playground. But my father was first, and never shall I forget the stentorian thunder of his tones. Seizing in each hand one of my lesser persecutors, he shook them like thistles before the wind, while time after time, breaking into his highest falsetto, he overtopped even my most piercing note. Colourless and stricken, a little group of masters stood huddled against the wall of the house, while an ever-growing stream of neighbours and local tradesmen began to throng every inch of the asphalt. Then, with a final and supreme imprecation, he flung the two ruffians into the midst of their fellows, and clasping me to his bosom, clove his way through the now vociferously applauding multitude. It was perhaps the greatest moment of his career, but like myself he had to pay the penalty of it, and for the following two weeks we were confined in adjacent bedrooms, while my mother had to wait upon us night and day. Afterwards, shaken as he was, he had a third interview with Mr Lorton, insisting upon and obtaining a public apology as the only alternative to legal proceedings.

Chapter Six

I have frequently been asked, and I have but little doubt that hosts of my readers will put the same query to me, why I did not, after such an experience, transfer my attendance to another school. And I ought to say at once, perhaps, that both my father and myself were strongly disposed to this course. Having regard to the facts, however, that Hopkinson House School was the only one in the neighbourhood for sons of gentlemen; that my moral position had now been defined there beyond any possibility of doubt; that the apologies elicited would probably secure me in the future from any further corporal interference; and that both Simeon and Silas Whey had expressed their horror at my treatment – in view of these facts, we came to the conclusion that, for the present at any rate, I had better remain there. That it could never be the same to me was of course the case. But then my hopes had not been extravagant. And although, as I have indicated, my boyhood had been ruthlessly plucked from me like a geranium in full bud, my early young manhood found me securer than ever in the approval of a wise and discerning Providence. Apart from an occasional boil, too, and a somewhat intractable and disfiguring affection known as acne, my health was giving rise to less anxiety than for some time past, and I have always looked back on the next two years as amongst the happiest of my life.

Necessarily thrown, as the result of what had happened, very largely upon my own resources, I was agreeably surprised to find that these were even richer and more varied than I had supposed; and I frequently walked, on a Saturday afternoon, as far as Dulwich or Blackheath, thoroughly contented with the company of none other than myself. What was my joy, too, to discover, a couple of weeks after my fifteenth birthday, that my voice had broken into a full-toned bass that promised to be even more powerful than my father's; and many a long hour did we spend at the harmonium together in friendly competition over our favourite hymns. Though he was rather more accurate than myself in the matter of tune, in the matter of time there was little to choose between us, while in the actual volume of sound produced I was soon my father's equal, if not his superior.

Nor was singing our only mutual occupation, for once a month, thanks to my father's generosity, we would journey to such a place of instructional interest as the Tower of London or Sir John Soane's Museum. We even visited, I remember, the National Gallery of Art, with its remarkable collection of hand-painted pictures; and I can still recall the delicacy with which my father would intervene to shelter me from any that contained an undraped female figure.

Perhaps our happiest times, however, were those spent with Nature during my father's annual fortnight's holiday, when we would usually procure lodgings at some such salubrious resort as Clacton-on-Sea or Cliftonville, near Margate. Here we would abandon ourselves to the contemplation of the waves, and here, under my father's skilful tuition, I became quite an adept at an entrancing pursuit less well known, I think, than it should be.

Consisting in the first place of the selection of a flat-shaped stone — itself often a gleeful and difficult task — it then becomes the object of the participators in the game to propel this seawards across the surface of the ocean. Being heavier than water, it would naturally be supposed that at the first impact with the latter the stone would sink; and indeed, if projected by an unskilled player, this is what usually eventuates. As I was happy to demonstrate, however, to our Sunday School mistresses only last year at Southend, in the hands of a careful and experienced performer this is by no means necessarily the case. Supporting the stone, with its flatter surface downwards, on the flexed middle finger of the thrower's hand, his (or her) fore-finger should lie along its circumference, the thumb gently resting on its superior surface. It should then be so cast as to travel horizontally, its flat surface parallel to the surface of the water, with the surprising result that, when at last it drops, it bounces into the air again and proceeds onwards. Nay, it may even, in the hands of the most expert, repeat this process two or three times, to the intense and delighted fascination of those who have been privileged to witness him.

Not lacking in the element of competition, yet devoid of all possibility of personal danger, affording healthful exercise, but at the same time immune from the perils of over-exertion, it has always seemed strange to me that, up to the present, it has played so small a part in our national life. An island community, here if anywhere is a diversion that should surely appeal to us; and I for one should rejoice to see the day when, instead of the football ground and the tennis pitch, our coasts should be thronged with eager young men and women enjoying this hygienic and innocent pastime.

Nor did we confine ourselves, while at the seaside, merely to terrestrial amusement, and we would frequently indulge, for perhaps a quarter of an hour, in the enjoyable practice of pedal immersion. Wholly precluded, of course, for constitutional reasons, from the fuller development of this art involved in swimming, we nevertheless found this to be a most laughable and even exciting occupation; and I can recall at least two occasions when, owing to a momentary inadversion, our rolled-up trousers became partially submerged. A short run home, however, a cup of hot milk, and immediate retirement to bed sufficed, in both instances, to protect us from any untoward results.

With my two friends, also, Simeon and Silas Whey, I had many hours of fruitful companionship. Equally segregated with myself from the majority of their schoolfellows, though less upon moral and intellectual than purely physical grounds, they were yet earnest and high-minded lads with many notably endearing qualities. Reticent to an extreme, partly, in the case of

Silas, owing to an initial difficulty in articulating anything at all, and in the case of Simeon, owing to a kind of laryngeal click from which he is still unfortunately a sufferer, they appeared to find a comfort in my own natural eloquence that I was only too glad to bestow upon them. In return for this, their ample pocket-money was always entirely at my disposal, and many a pound of toffee and Turkish delight was I able to enjoy at their expense. Like myself unaddicted to athletics, and thereby preserved from its associated vices, they would saunter for hours with me discussing some favourite Bible character or humming in unison some well-known hymn; and we were further united, if that were possible, in our eventual confirmation by the self-same Bishop.

Nevertheless, as I have said, it was chiefly upon myself that I had to depend for company; and in my walks abroad, my studies of the shop-windows, and my exploration of the neighbouring churches, my closest comrade was myself, and I can honestly say that I have never regretted it. Nor must it be supposed that the hours so spent were entirely devoid of legitimate adventure. On two or three occasions, for instance, I was abruptly addressed by some surprised or suspicious verger, and once, owing to ignorance of its usual closing hours, I was incarcerated in a local cemetery. Confined by railings too lofty to scale and too narrowly approximated to permit egress, for a few moments the prospects were sufficiently black to cause a sensible quickening of my pulse. A felicitous remark, however, addressed to an under-gardener, secured my exit by a private gate, and I hurried home, not without relief but none the worse for my little mischance.

Nor shall I forget the thrill, perhaps a trifle guilty, with which I discovered, soon after I was sixteen, how to descend from a vehicle in motion without the sacrifice of an erect position. Hitherto, like my father, when travelling by tram or omnibus, I had always insisted upon complete immobility prior both to entrance into and departure from one of these public conveyances; and many a conductor had been reported by us both for failing to secure the requisite lack of motion. Upon my sixteenth birthday, however, perceiving that the omnibus in which I was journeying could not be brought to a standstill at the desired position, I decided to alight from it notwithstanding and boldly descended from its posterior step.

Naturally leaving this at right angles, what was my rather rueful amazement to discover myself, in the next instant, lying upon my side in the roadway. At first I imagined that I must have stepped upon something slippery or that some such article must have been adhering to my footwear. But a minute examination both of this and the roadway failed to reveal any such cause. Completely baffled, I made a second attempt, but with an equally discomforting result, and time after time, in spite of my utmost efforts, I was the victim of a similar loss of equilibrium. Many a less determined and timider lad would indeed have given up the venture, and again I ought to confess, perhaps, in view of municipal regulations, that my pertinacity was not wholly defensible.

Robbed of candour, however, such a record as the present would lose the greater part of its spiritual value;

and while I am prepared to admit that, in this particular instance, my youthful conduct may have been open to misjudgement, I cannot concede that it was in any degree incompatible with the highest expression of the Xtian character. Refusing to be cast down, therefore, save in the most literal sense, I continued dauntlessly with my efforts, to be rewarded at last with a final success no less gratifying than entire. Failing to remain upright in departing from the moving vehicle either at right angles to it or with my back towards the driver, I found that by *facing in the same direction* I could not only descend from it with greater immunity, but that by *running after it*, as it were, for two or three steps, I could do so with complete integrity. Needless to say, having acquired this knowledge, I only made use of it in an occasional emergency, and for some years now, owing to declining success, I have discontinued the practice altogether.

With the unfolding of my seventeenth year, however, I was definitely approaching the great problems of adult life, and much of my time now began to be occupied with the contemplation of my future career. Thanks to the tempered foresight of my father, a firm believer, as a rule, in unlimited families, in the exceptional circumstances of his own case he had refrained from further parentage. On his demise, therefore, as he had given me to understand, I should inherit some two thousand pounds, this being the amount to which his insurance and savings would by then probably have accrued. Should my mother survive him, I should, of course, be expected, and would gladly, as I assured him, make her some allowance. But her health was so precarious as to render this sacrifice a very improbable necessity.

Devoid of anxiety, therefore, as to ultimate no less than immediate penury, I could afford to regard the future with an adequate deliberation, and I need scarcely say, perhaps, that the Church of England was the subject of my first and most prolonged consideration. Financially inadequate as were even its highest rewards, I was yet so adapted to its every need that both my father and myself would have been willing to overlook this very serious disadvantage. But to become ordained presupposed an examination, and I had been seriously handicapped in this particular respect by a proven disability, probably hereditary in origin, to demonstrate my culture in so confined a form.

For a similar reason, even had I been attracted to it, the profession of Medicine would have been unavailable, while from that of the Law, nobler in every way, I was equally precluded. For some time, however, we canvassed very carefully the strong claims of Diplomacy, for which in many ways, as my father agreed with me, I was most admirably fitted. And I am still convinced that both as attaché and ambassador I should have found congenial and Xtian employment. Unhappily, however, such a career involved the acquirement of the French language, with attendant dangers, to which my father could not persuade himself to expose me. Whether he was right in this is perhaps open to argument, and I have since met several apparently devout men who have not only spoken this tongue with reported fluency, but have deliberately sojourned in the country of its origin. Personally, however, while reluctant to condemn them, I must confess to sharing my father's views, and I am happy in the knowledge that the vicar of my parish holds precisely the same opinion. Abandoning Diplomacy, therefore, we considered the Consolidated Water Board, in which my father, of course, had considerable influence. But here, as in the Church of England, the emoluments were unsatisfactory, while the spiritual opportunities, of course, were far more restricted.

Thus step by step, as though by the hand of Providence – and indeed, as my father said, it could have been by no other hand – we were slowly led to the conclusion that in some branch of Commerce lay my future destiny. Requiring no previous examinations, with liberal, nay, illimitable, monetary possibilities, this was the field — the highest, perhaps, of all – that was now unfolded before our gaze. For a few moments, I remember, we sat there speechless, one on each side of the parlour table. Then my father rose and stood for another few moments with his right hand resting on the harmonium. In his face there was a great joy, not unmixed with solemnity. His eyes looked beyond me out towards eternity. Indeed it was to eternity that he addressed himself.

'Augustus,' he said, 'my son Augustus – a Xtian tradesman, preferably wholesale.'

My mother came in to announce the supper. But almost impatiently he motioned her aside.

'Oh, can't you see,' he cried, 'that we're standing on Pisgah?'

For a moment, not comprehending him, she stared at

his feet. Then very softly she withdrew, and he came toward me with outstretched hands.

'A Xtian magnate,' he said, 'a commercial Xtian – what better could I have desired for you?'

Impulsively I kissed him, perhaps a little too impulsively. But he scarcely flinched as he received the impact, merely remarking that, upon the next day, he would present me with my first razor. Nor did he fail to do so, partly reminded by myself and partly by the appearance, early the next morning, of a slight but painful urticaria or nettle-rash in the region of our most vehement facial adjustment. But that was a penalty, as he several times assured me, that many a father would have been glad to pay, and one that yielded, in less than a fortnight, to an inunction embracing the oxide of zinc.

Chapter Seven

A further vision is vouchsafed to us by Providence. Mr
Chrysostom Lorton and the sources of his wealth. The debt owed
to me by Mr Septimus Lorton. Interview with Mr and Mrs
Septimus Lorton. Mr Septimus Lorton's disgraceful attitude.
My father is compelled to be frank with him. What I discovered
in Greenwich Park.

Manifestly as it had been Providence that had thus
revealed to us the general sphere of my future activities,
it was no less clearly the same beneficent Agency that
determined their actual channel; and it has always
seemed to me peculiarly appropriate that the particular
enterprise with which I was to be first connected should
have been suggested to my father during the process of
family prayers.

This took place, according to our usual custom,
immediately after the conclusion of our evening meal,
and consisted of the singing by my father and myself of
two or three hymns or sacred choruses, followed by the
reading on the part of my father of a chapter of Holy
Scripture, the whole being concluded by one of those
extemporary prayers in the composition of which my
father was so skilled. For the purposes of the Scripture
reading the volume generally used was a large Bible
inherited by my father, but on the evening in question,
owing to an accident with some stewed fruit, this was
absent at a neighbouring bookbinder's. My father had

therefore borrowed with my glad permission my copy of the Lorton Bible for Schools, and it was in opening this that he caught sight of the words 'eighteenth edition' on the first page.

That something had perturbed him was instantly apparent both to my mother and myself, not only on account of the sudden tremor that became visible in his left hand, but of the extraordinary rapidity with which he read the appointed chapter, and the verbal errors that consequently ensued. His subsequent prayer, too, was so brief that we were scarcely upon our knees before he had leapt to his feet again, and my mother and myself, indeed, were still kneeling when he began to expound the idea that had been vouchsafed to him.

'I have it,' he cried. 'It's just been sent to me. Chrysostom Lorton. That's the man. Eighteen editions – that's what his Bible's gone into, and none of the authors with any royalty rights!'

Nor was that all, for in addition, as I have said, to being the elder brother of Mr Septimus Lorton, he was not only the proprietor of the well-known *Beulah*, perhaps the most popular of weekly religious journals, but his *Peeping Up Series for Children*, devotional stories with coloured illustrations, were familiar objects upon the nursery book-shelves of every evangelical household. Moreover, he was the medium through which were issued to the world many millions of hortatory pamphlets, while the counters of his show-room in Paternoster Row were heaped with every kind of Protestant literature.

Such, then, was the man and such the undertaking, not only Xtian, but lucrative, that by a chance gesture, or so it might have seemed, now stood beckoning before us; and it was only necessary, as my father justly said, for his brother Septimus to do the rest. But would he? I was at first doubtful. A weak man, he was also inert. And it did not, of course, follow that because he used his brother's Bible he was on intimate or influential terms with him. This much was clear, however, that as the oldest pupil in his school, and in view of the treatment that I had received from his subordinates, he was under an obligation to me that neither my father nor myself could morally allow ourselves to remit. And although for reasons that I have already mentioned I had not advanced from my original class, in the strictly ethical sense, by his own admission, I was *facile princeps*.*

'A good boy,' said Mr Lorton, 'a very, very good boy, or shall we say, now that he has begun to shave, an extremely admirable young man.'

This was upon the next evening, the penultimate evening of my last term at school, when both my father and myself were sitting in Mr Lorton's study for the purpose indicated above.

'It is useless to deny, of course,' my father had said, 'that we have been seriously disappointed in your school, or to suggest that either my son or myself will be able to look back upon it with approval. Nor can I profess to be wholly convinced as to the necessity that you have so often explained to me of promoting your pupils from class to class according to the results of an examination. At the same time I am open-minded enough to recognize that this method has the sanction of custom, and to forbear from arraigning you for the consequently meagre

* Easily first.

position that my son still occupies in your establishment. Refusing to accept the standard, I can afford to ignore its results. But of this, Mr Lorton, I am completely confident – that if the index had been a moral or religious one, my boy Augustus would have been second to none.

Here my father paused for a moment to expectorate some phlegm, and it was then that Mr Lorton used the words I have quoted.

'A good boy,' he said, as his wife entered the room, 'a very, very good boy, or shall we say, now that he has begun to shave, an extremely admirable young man.'

A heavily-constructed woman of immense height, with prominent cheek-bones and a bovine chin, it was generally understood that Mr Lorton had selected her chiefly on account of her income. And neither my father nor myself had ever been able to detect in her the least sign of intelligence. Happily her intrusion, however, was but momentary, and my father was able once more to proceed.

'I am obliged to you for your tribute,' he said, 'and if, as you must surely admit, my son's influence in your school has been inestimable, you will the more readily agree with me in adopting a reciprocal attitude towards the important question of his future employment.'

As we both observed, Mr Lorton's expression changed a little. But his voice retained its professional amiability.

'Oh, precisely,' he said, 'precisely, although you must understand, of course, that my influence is strictly limited.'

'Nevertheless,' said my father, 'I am depending on its exertion to the utmost boundary of its capacity. And I should be glad to learn what openings you have in view for one to whom so admittedly you are a debtor.'

At this point Mrs Lorton returned and took up a position on her husband's left flank. Mr Lorton glanced at her before replying.

'Well, of course,' he said, 'the problem is a somewhat difficult one.'

'It would be easier,' said Mrs Lorton, 'if we were an employment agency.'

My father bowed.

'That I fully appreciate,' he said. 'But I may at least assume, I trust, that you have considered the problem.'

'Oh, deeply,' said Mr Lorton, 'very deeply, in fact I ought to say, perhaps, profoundly.'

My father leaned back, folding his arms.

'Then may I inquire,' he asked, 'with what result?'

Again Mr Lorton glanced at his wife. But her slab-like face remained unstirred.

'Well, I can hardly say,' he replied, 'that as yet – er – we have come to a definite conclusion. The moral qualities, you see, though extremely valuable –'

'For ultimate salvation,' said my father, 'they are essential.'

'Oh, of course,' said Mr Lorton, 'of course. But in the meantime, you know, and taken by themselves –' He paused for a moment, and then his face brightened. 'Have you ever thought,' he said, 'of making your son a missionary?'

A sort of sigh emanated from his wife.

'In a warm country,' she said, 'a long way off?'

Mr Lorton nodded.

'Healthy but remote,' he said, 'where his moral

enthusiasm could have full play?'

'And where his personal appearance,' said Mrs Lorton, 'could scarcely fail to be such a protection to him?'

'Quite so,' said Mr Lorton. 'I can conceive of no one eating dear Augustus.'

Mrs Lorton smiled not unkindly.

'No one at all,' she said, 'not even the most debased.'

Afterwards, as we discovered, these remarks lacked sincerity. But for the moment we were not ungrateful. Colouring with pleasure my father lifted his hand.

'I am again obliged to you,' he said, 'for your tribute.'

Mr Lorton rose to his feet, evidently under the impression that the interview had ended.

'Oh, not at all,' he said, 'not at all, we are only too happy to have been of any assistance.'

He moved towards the door. But my father motioned him back. Somewhat less agreeably, I thought, he sat down again. Allowing him a moment for this, my father then proceeded.

'Sensible as I am,' he said, 'both of the justice, and I may say discernment, of your suggestion, neither on financial nor hygienic grounds am I able to entertain it; and indeed in its main outlines the province of my son's future has already been delineated for us. Second to none in my admiration of the noble calling to which you have referred, surely they are nobler who have created the means by which our missionaries subsist, and who, of the wealth that their efforts have amassed, continue to support these emissaries of religion. It is therefore to Commerce that my son has been called, but in his first introduction to this sacred field, we have only thought it right to afford you the opportunity of being the possible instrument of Providence.'

'I see,' said Mr Lorton. 'That is very kind of you.'

'Take away the number,' said his wife, 'that you first thought of.'

My father stared at her. But she appeared to be in a kind of stupor, and it seemed more merciful to avert his eyes.

'It has, in fact, occurred to us,' he said, 'or rather to me – for it was to me personally that the idea was vouchsafed – that your brother Chrysostom would be glad to hear that my son's services were now available.'

For two or three moments Mr Lorton seemed to struggle for breath. Then he made a meaningless sound like that of a small animal.

'My brother C – Chrysostom?' he said at last. 'But in what capacity would you propose to offer your son?'

My father smiled somewhat dryly.

'I should hardly have thought offer,' he said, 'was the right word.'

Mrs Lorton looked at her husband.

'He means that dear Augustus,' she said, 'would allow Chrysostom to approach him.'

'Provided,' said my father, 'that he gave sufficient assurances. Of course we should look forward to an eventual partnership.'

'And not to succession?' asked Mrs Lorton.

'Only in the event,' said my father, 'of Mr Chrysostom's decease.'

Mr Lorton wiped his forehead.

'That's most considerate,' he said, 'most con-siderate.'

Mor Chrysostom Borton

'Then perhaps I can rely,' said my father, 'on your taking immediate steps to arrange an interview for us with your brother.'

But Mr Lorton shook his head.

'I'm very sorry,' he replied. 'But that's quite impossible. For, in the first place, my brother's business is a very complicated and peculiar one, and in the second I regret to say that I have absolutely no influence with him. In fact – er – well, to tell the truth, any testimonial from me would be worse than useless.'

'Oh, worse,' said Mrs Lorton, 'much worse. And besides, he has no vacancies.'

For perhaps a quarter of a minute there was a dead silence, and then very slowly my father rose to his feet.

'So I am to understand,' he said, 'that you entirely refuse to approach your brother on my son's behalf?'

With a pitiable gesture Mr Lorton shrugged his shoulders, and the clock on the mantelpiece made an insolent crowing noise. Trembling, but composed, my father swept it to the floor together with several of its adjacent ornaments. Then very quietly, but with increasing emphasis, he began to address Mr Lorton. It was a painful task. It is always a painful task to confront such a character with its own portrait. But it was a duty from which, I am proud to say, I never knew my father to shrink. Nor did he cease, on the present occasion, until the last iota of it had been discharged, though such, as I have shown, was his verbal economy that this was completed in fifteen minutes. Then with his hand resting upon my shoulder, for he was still the taller by two and a half inches, we turned our backs, as we thought for ever, upon Mr and Mrs Septimus Lorton.

I have said for ever. But though, as the event proved, this was a misjudgement on both our parts, it must not be assumed that either my father or myself had lost his self-confidence. For the moment, it was true, the path seemed obstructed, the vision obscured, the end denied. But neither of us doubted that, by means yet unrevealed, I should be brought at last to the destined haven, although, as I must admit, neither of us foresaw the tremendous speed with which this would be accomplished.

Such was the case, however, for when brooding alone, upon the very next evening, in Greenwich Park, a familiar voice pierced my consciousness and suddenly awakened my every faculty. It was a warm but cloudy April dusk, and I was sitting upon a seat under a large chestnut tree, when I began to hear again, to my disgust and astonishment, the detested voice of Mr Septimus Lorton. Rapidly withdrawing myself behind the tree, I then observed him to be approaching my seat, evidently engrossed in his conversation with a medium-sized female who was accompanying him. For a moment, as was only natural, I resolved to transport myself as far as possible from his neighbourhood. But by some impulse – I realize now, of course, that this could only have had one origin – I merely performed perhaps a quarter of a revolution round the commanding trunk of the chestnut tree. By this manoeuvre, not, I think, uningenious, I thus concealed myself from his vision, while at the same time conferring upon myself such possible advantages as might accrue from observation. Nor was the event to prove me unjustified. For hardly had he arrived at the seat that I had vacated when he proceeded, accompanied

70

by his companion, himself to sit down upon it.

Being a slow runner my position now was one of the extremest peril, and in the event of detection, I could only have relied upon my happily exceptional vocal powers. But a closer inspection of Mr Lorton's companion and something in the tones in which he was addressing her combined in bidding me hold my ground entirely regardless of personal danger. Indeed from the beginning, I think, it was less the physical than the moral contingencies that disturbed me. For I had instantly recognized, to my profound discomfort, that the person accompanying him *was not Mrs Septimus Lorton*. A woman of much slenderer and more graceful build, she had a pink complexion and hazel eyes, with a rather large but conceivably alluring mouth, and a considerable quantity of yellowish hair. Her name, it appeared, was Nina, the i being pronounced as if it were an e, and it was quickly apparent to me that, for the first time, I was in the presence of the gravest human vice. Nor have I ever, perhaps, entirely recovered from the enormous shock of that discovery. For though I had been aware, of course, from my studies of Holy Scripture, that such things had occurred in the Middle East, and had even deduced from contemporary newspapers their occasional survival in the British Islands, I had never dreamed it possible that here, in a public park in the Xtian London of my own experience, a married man could thus openly sit with his arm round a female who was not his wife.

Trembling all over, I was afraid for two or three moments that I was about to relapse into unconsciousness, and that I did not do so I can only attribute to the amazing discovery that followed. For no sooner had Mr Lorton taken his seat than the petrifying fact became manifest that his fellow-criminal was not only married herself, but was *actually the wife of his brother Chrysostom.** Afterwards, as was inevitable perhaps, I utterly broke down, but not until I had made full notes of their conversation, learned that Mrs Chrysostom was supposed to be out shopping, and observed them kiss one another several times. Then, pale and distraught, blinded with tears, and scarcely indeed able to suppress my sobs, I hurried home, and within less than an hour had buried my face in my father's waistcoat.

'Oh, father,' I cried, 'father,' and though he had mis-interpreted my convulsions, I shall never forget the tenderness with which he signalled to my mother to fetch a basin as quickly as possible. Nor was he less sympathetic when I had succeeded in convincing him that my paroxysms were spiritual rather than gastric, for smoothing my hair with his unoccupied hand, he at once readjusted my head to its former position.

'My poor boy,' he said, 'my poor Augustus. Tell me what's happened. Take your time. There, there now. I've sent your mother away. But she's left the basin here in case.'

'Oh, sin,' I cried, 'sin – unbelievable sin in Greenwich Park.'

I felt my father's abdomen give a violent heave.

'In Greenwich Park?' he said. 'Never!'

'Oh, yes,' I cried, 'yes. Would that it were no. But it was not no.'

My father bent over me, patting my head.

* I am happy to say that this pernicious family is now completely extinct.

'My poor boy,' he said. 'What sort of sin?'

'Oh, the worst,' I said, 'the worst. It was Mr Lorton and Mrs Chrysostom.'

'Good heavens,' said my father, 'Mr Lorton?'

'Mr Septimus,' I said, 'and Mrs Chrysostom.'

'But what were they doing?' asked my father.

Burning all over, I replied that they had been kissing.

'Kissing,' he said, 'kissing? You mean to tell me you saw them kissing?'

'Oh, father,' I said, 'several times, with mutual expressions of passionate regard.'

I had now reared my head from the lower part of his waistcoat, and it would have been hard to say which of us was the deeper scarlet. Then my father covered his eyes.

'Mutual expressions?' he whispered. 'Do you remember them?'

With a shaking hand I offered him my pocketbook.

'They are there,' I said. 'I wrote them down.'

Like a tornado he tore them from my grasp.

'My darling,' he read. 'Oh, Septimus. Give me another. Well just one. My only darling. Light of my heart. Do you know what your lips are like? No, tell me.'

Then a great light shone in my father's eyes.

'Providence has delivered them,' he said, 'into our hands.'

For a moment I was silent. Then I rose to my feet.

'I had rather thought,' I said, 'that might be the case.'

'Oh, it is,' said my father. 'It is. Do you remember those beautiful words of David's, "the righteous shall rejoice when he seeth the vengeance: he shall wash his feet in the blood of the wicked"?'

'Not only do I remember them,' I said, 'but had you not quoted them, I should certainly have done so myself.'

'We'll wash them tonight,' said my father. 'Put on your cap. No, it would perhaps be better to wear your bowler,' and five minutes later we were standing once more on the front-door step of Hopkinson House.

Chapter Eight

Second interview with Mr Septimus Lorton. But now the tables are turned. A pitiful exhibition. My father demands guarantees. He will write a letter to Mrs Chrysostom Lorton. My father's ordeal. When it was dark.

Save that it became the means so strangely selected for my early entrance into Xtian commerce, I do not propose to linger over the comparatively brief but effective interview that ensued. At first refused admission, the words Greenwich Park sent as a message by the servant sufficed to bring Mr Lorton hastily but reluctantly and unaccompanied to the front door. From there he conveyed us to one of the smaller and more distant schoolrooms, and it soon became obvious, in spite of his tentative denials, and even more despicable evasions, that my father and myself were the complete masters of the situation. It was true, of course, that he tried to temporize with the pathetic bravado of the exposed sinner.

'But even if it were the case,' he said, 'which I am not prepared to admit, that I was in Greenwich Park with Mrs Chrysostom, do you suppose that, were I to deny it, my brother would believe you for a moment?'

Fulfilled as he was with a Xtian indignation, my father was unable to suppress a smile.

'I imagine that at least,' he said, 'he would be interested in my son's knowledge that she was supposed to be shopping in Kensington.'

Mr Septimus Lorton protruded the tip of his tongue in a vain endeavour to moisten his lips.

'And he would also be interested,' I said, 'to meet the lame newspaper-seller from whom she obtained change for ten shillings.'

My father nodded.

'That cannot often happen,' he said, 'and my son tells me that the man picked up one of her gloves.'

'Yes,' I said, 'and followed her into the station with it, where she gave him a sixpence, and he called her a pretty lady.'

My father looked thoughtfully at the tips of his fingers.

'From which I infer,' he said, 'that he could probably identify her.'

Mr Lorton passed one of his hands over the pale green surface of his cheek.

'But, my dear sir,' he said, 'my dear sir, even suppose, I say, that without – er – prejudice, Mrs Chrysostom had so far honoured me as to accompany me for a walk in the park you mention, surely that is not necessarily an indiscreet act in view of the fact that I am her husband's brother.'

Again my father smiled.

'But a brother, you must remember, whose testimonial would be worse than useless.'

For a moment Mr Lorton glanced from side to side with the bestial expression of a hunted rat. Then he spoke huskily, after licking his lips again and listening for a second or two over his left shoulder.

'Perhaps I was rather hasty,' he said, 'rather hasty. In fact, I had – er – already begun to reconsider that.'

'I am happy to hear it,' said my father.

'In fact,' said Mr Lorton, 'I think something could be done.'

My father bowed again. He was no longer smiling. I had seldom, indeed, seen him look so grave.

'For the sake of your school,' he said, 'to say nothing of your soul, and for the sake of your brother's business, I sincerely hope so.'

'Oh, I think so,' said Mr Lorton, 'I think so. Now, let me see. How could I be most helpful?'

My father cleared his throat.

'Deeply as I am inclined,' he said, 'to expose this iniquity to the uttermost, and irreparable as has been its injury to my son's sensibilities, I am yet prepared to concede you the opportunity of retaining at least the semblance of your good name. But for my son I must claim every guarantee. Upon my son's future your own is dependent.'

I dare not record that Mr Lorton smiled. Let me rather say that he exposed his incisors.

'Dear Augustus,' he said, 'I'm sure he'll succeed. I'll send a line to my brother's wife.'

My father's expression never changed.

'Do you apprehend then,' he inquired, 'that she can secure him the requisite position?'

'Far more probably,' said Mr Lorton, 'than I. My – er – Mr Chrysostom Lorton is deeply attached to her.'

My father's silence was perhaps more eloquent than any merely verbal condemnation.

'I – er – I'll write tonight,' said Mr Lorton.

'Perhaps,' said my father, 'you'd be so kind as to give us Mrs Chrysostom Lorton's address.'

Mr Lorton hesitated.

'Oh – er – certainly,' he said. 'Paternoster Towers, Enfield.'

My father made a note of this in his diary.

'We shall call upon her,' he said, 'tomorrow at noon.'

Mr Lorton emitted a sort of gargling sound.

'I – er – I'll tell her,' he said. 'She'll be delighted.'

Strong in the Lord, therefore, and indeed in comparatively good spirits considering the vileness with which we had been brought into contact, we returned home to a belated but none the less substantial meal; and it was not until this had been absorbed and my mother was in the scullery, cleansing the dishes that had contained it, that my father referred again to the interview that had been arranged for the following day.

'Although it seemed wise,' he said, 'to suggest to that creature that both you and I would be present at it, I am afraid that my obligations to the Consolidated Water Board will, in reality, prevent me from being there, and that you must be prepared therefore, my dear Augustus, to face that female alone.'

I bowed my head.

'I pray that you may trust me,' I said.

With a slightly increased colour my father rose to his feet.

'I have no doubt of it,' he said. 'But at the same time – at the same time – oh, Augustus, Augustus!'

Deeply moved, he advanced two or three paces and leaned heavily against the harmonium.

'You see, my boy,' he continued – at what a cost I could only afterward guess – 'with this interview you will be definitely entering upon a new and most perilous phase of experience. For the first time – I must ask you to turn down the lamp – for the first time, as a marriageable adult, you will be called upon to encounter, face to face, a woman of fierce and unbridled passions.'

Here he paused for a moment and I could feel the floor shaking.

'Oh, father,' I cried. 'Can I not spare you?'

'No, no,' he said. 'I must see it through.'

I bent forward to steady the lamp, and at the same time I turned it lower.

'Mind the wick,' he said.

'Oh, father,' I cried, 'do you mean that she may want to kiss me?'

'Oh, Augustus,' he said, 'or even more.'

'Oh, father,' I cried. 'Is there anything more?'

He swallowed once or twice.

'Oh, Augustus,' he said.

I fear this chapter must remain unfinished.

Chapter Nine

*Effect upon my father of his disclosure. My Xtian confidence in
journeying to Enfield. Paternoster Towers and its mistress.
Unfortunate detachment of my posterior trouser-buttons.
Triumphant success of my interview. A kindly parlourmaid and
her male friend. I secure a position under Mr Chrysostom
Lorton. Melancholy death of Silas Whey.*

Profoundly, and indeed permanently, as it had shaken
him – when I turned up the lamp again my father was
an old man – I cannot say that the substance of his
communication was entirely unfamiliar to me, or that I
had not been aware, to a certain extent, of a new
significance attaching to my person. Appreciably over
five feet in height, with a pectoral girth of twenty-six
inches, my abdominal measurement (fully clothed of
course) was but little less than a yard, and for some time
I had been unable to help noticing that I was not
unattractive to the opposite sex. I had, in fact, deemed
it advisable to inform Emily Smith, who, as I have said,
was somewhat my senior, that while I was still agreeable
to remain her companion, there could be no question
between us of ultimate matrimony; and I had several
times discussed with Simeon and Silas Whey the
qualities to be demanded from a possible wife.

Even had I not been fortified, therefore, with the
details, imparted at such a price to me by my father, I
should not have felt myself wholly unequipped in

confronting Mrs Chrysostom Lorton; and, as it was, I made the journey to Enfield serene in the knowledge of my instructed manhood. This was the more fortunate in that, devoid of anxiety, I was enabled to profit very fully from an expedition considerably the most involved that I had ever engaged upon unaccompanied.

Nothing would have been easier, for instance, than, dazed by its magnitude, to have wandered for hours in Liverpool Street Station, whereas a few courteous and clearly-phrased questions soon led my footsteps to the appropriate platform. Similarly, had I been engrossed with a fearful apprehension of the ordeal that awaited me, I might have been blind to the interesting objects that presented themselves to my carriage window; whereas I was moved to pity and apprehension by the rough streets of Bethnal Green, pricked to audible curiosity by the uncommon nomenclature of Seven Sisters, agreeably reminded, at Bruce Grove, of the well-known Caledonian monarch, and so overcome by mirth, as we drew into Lower Edmonton, at a sudden recollection of John Gilpin that an elderly female who was sitting opposite me hastily left the compartment.

I was able to observe, too, with satisfaction, the busy and prosperous aspect of Enfield, and although, as I drew near to the mansion of Mr Chrysostom Lorton, I was naturally a little sobered by the imminence of my task, I was gratified to perceive in Paternoster Towers a concrete testimony to the worth of his enterprise. Solidly constructed of red brick and surrounded by well-trimmed lawns and flower-beds, it was further adhered to by a couple of large conservatories and approached by a broad, gravelled drive. Nor was I less satisfied by the humble and respectful demeanour of the good-looking parlourmaid who opened the door, and who had proceeded, having taken my hat and stick, to admit me to her mistress's boudoir.

'Mrs Lorton,' she said, 'will be down in a minute.'

'I thank you,' I replied. 'I will await her arrival.'

Favourably as I had been impressed, however, it must not be assumed that I had in any degree relaxed my guard; and though I was aware, of course, that I held every advantage, I made a rapid survey of the contents of the room.

Of no great size, it had evidently been furnished to minister almost entirely to the senses, and it was perhaps not surprising that I was unable to discern a single text upon its walls. Upon a parquet floor polished to a degree that was almost lascivious in its smoothness, elaborate table-legs stood reflected and a voluptuous rug or two solicited the feet. Upon the mantelpiece stood an oval mirror, indecently surrounded by likenesses of Cupid, and beside it a nude female, fashioned in bronze, was extracting a thorn from her left calf. Flushing involuntarily, I turned away from these only to observe upon a French-looking writing-table a large photograph of an elderly man, pathetically signed 'Your aff. Chrysostom'. Beneath this, in a confusion that was probably characteristic, lay a half-finished letter to somebody called Loo-Loo and several others addressed to 'Dearest Nina' that I did not hesitate to peruse. Most of these, as I discovered, were but little more than the vapid productions of obvious worldlings. But two were invitations to card parties and one, to my horror, contained the word 'blasted'.

This was the one, indeed, upon which I was engaged when the door of the room was abruptly thrown open with a lack of refinement that I ought perhaps to have expected, but that for a moment completely unnerved me. In fact, it did more. For in the effort to recover myself the rug upon which I was standing slid across the floor, leaving behind it not only the upper and middle but the lower middle portions of my frame. Poised in mid-air, my feet having accompanied the rug, I was entirely unable to support these, and was obliged in consequence to assume with the extremest suddenness a sedentary position upon the parquet. Nor was that all. For when, at the third attempt, I succeeded in once more standing upright, the left of my two posterior trouser-buttons fell with a sharp metallic sound upon the floor. Here it paused for a moment, and then standing upon its circumference followed the rug in the direction of Mrs Lorton.

'Dear me,' she said, 'I'm afraid I interrupted you. Is this your button?'

She stooped and picked it up.

With a supreme effort, and despite the most poignant anguish, I regained command of myself and requested her to return it. Hardly had she done so, however, when there came a second metallic sound, and the comrade of the first button also rolled to her feet.

'Oh, dear,' she said, 'isn't that the other one? What do you suppose will happen now?'

Only those who have experienced the extreme discomfort of the simultaneous loss of both posterior trouser-buttons, and the consequent approach to the back of the neck of the bifurcation-point of the braces, will be able to appreciate the enormous handicap under which Providence had now seen fit to place me. In the manual effort, too, which became instantly necessary to prevent the downward corrugation of my trousers, the first button slipped from my grasp and again bounced upon the parquet.

'Oh, I say,' said Mrs Lorton, 'is this a new kind of game, or are you trying to put me at my ease?'

With a silent but powerful petition, I drew myself as erect as the circumstances permitted.

'It is neither a game,' I said, holding up my trousers, 'nor am I entering into personal relations with you. In fact, it is my duty to make it quite clear to you that you are no sort of temptation to me.'

Clad in some close-fitting fabric that exuded a most licentious scent, I could see at once that these well-chosen words had had a profound and immediate effect upon her. Turning her back on me, she emitted a hoarse gasp, and then collapsing upon the sofa, she lay there choking and convulsed in what appeared to be an attack of acute hysteria. Startled but unmoved, and still sustaining my trousers, I gravely awaited her recovery.

'Oh dear,' she said, wiping her eyes, and then after looking at me again, she collapsed once more. Then she sat up, fanning herself with her handkerchief.

'You must really forgive me,' she said, 'but you looked so stern.'

'I should scarcely have thought,' I replied, inclining my head a little, 'that as a Xtian gentleman you could have expected me to look otherwise.'

'Oh no,' she said, 'no, of course not. Just suppose – oh dear, oh dear.'

Then she wiped her eyes again.

'Wouldn't you be better sitting down?' she asked.

'I thank you,' I said. 'But I prefer to stand.'

She folded up her handkerchief and placed it in a small bag.

'Well, you know best,' she said. 'What do you want me to do?'

'I had imagined,' I said, 'that that had already been indicated to you by your fellow-accomplice, Mr Septimus Lorton.'

'I say,' she replied, 'you do use long words. Aren't you considered to be frightfully clever?'

I bowed again.

'In my own circle,' I said, 'I am not considered, I believe, to be unintelligent.'

'And so you want Chrys,' she said, 'to give you a job?'

'You are doubtless aware,' I replied, 'of the alternative.'

'You mean if he doesn't,' she said, 'you'll tell him about me and Septimus.'

'As a Xtian gentleman,' I said, 'it would become my duty.'

'I wonder what he'd say,' she said. 'When do you want to see him?'

'The sooner the better,' I said. 'I should prefer this afternoon.'

She rose to her feet.

'Then I'll have to write him a note,' she said. 'But it'll never do to mention poor Septimus.'

She crossed to the writing-table and began nibbling her pen.

'Of course it's rather difficult,' she said, 'to know

what to tell him.'

I bowed again, a trifle grimly perhaps.

'The way of transgressors,' I reminded her, 'is seldom easy.'

'No, I suppose not,' she said. 'How clever you are. Aren't they frightfully proud of you at home?'

'I trust,' I said, 'that I have deserved their affection.'

'Oh, I'm sure of it,' she replied. 'Now let me see.'

She frowned for a moment and then began writing in a peculiarly large and childish hand.

'Of course I'll have to tell him,' she said, 'that you were at Septimus's school, where you were frightfully struck with the Lorton Bible, but that you didn't like Septimus – that'll be sure to please him – and so you didn't ask him to help you.'

Her face began to brighten as she put this on paper, and I noticed that she was protruding the tip of her tongue.

'So you came here all by yourself, thinking he'd be at home, as it was the Easter holidays, and when you found he wasn't, you asked to see me instead, and I was most frightfully taken up with you.'

Here she made a blot, but observed that it didn't matter, and then pronounced each word as she slowly inscribed it.

'He seems a most lovable and religious young man, and I do hope you'll help him all you can. Cross, cross, cross – those are for kisses – your ever loving and devoted Nina.'

Then she handed me the letter.

'There you are,' she said. 'Now you'll know exactly what you'll have to tell him.'

Releasing one of my hands, I read it quickly but carefully and returned it to her without comment.

'Will it do?' she said.

'I can only hope,' I replied, 'that, for your own sake, madam, it will.'

She put it into an envelope and handed it back to me.

'Then I mustn't detain you,' she said, 'any longer.'

Nor did I wish to stay. But I was now face to face with a situation of the utmost difficulty. Growingly repugnant as was this woman's presence to me, and singularly complete as had been my moral triumph, both my posterior trouser-buttons were still lying upon the floor.

'Oh, I see,' she said, 'would you like to take them with you? I'll put them in an envelope and then you won't lose them.'

She accordingly did so, handing me the envelope, which I quickly took from her and placed in my pocket.

'You see, I'm afraid,' she said, 'that I could hardly trust myself to – to actually sew them on.'

I bowed to her coldly, ignoring the split infinitive.

'Nor should I have seen fit,' I said, 'to concede you the opportunity.'

Obviously shamed, she lowered her eyes, and to hide her confusion rang the bell, and I am glad to acknowledge that the entrance of the good-looking parlourmaid was not wholly unwelcome to me. Though but a menial, I had already discovered in her some of the most desirable female qualities, and I am happy to record that in a moment of acute anxiety, she played an humble but not unworthy part.

Mrs Lorton turned to her.

'Oh, Parker,' she said, 'poor Mr Carp has had a most unfortunate accident.'

Parker glanced at my hands.

'Yes, that's the trouble,' said Mrs Lorton. 'Isn't it awkward for him?'

Parker looked at me with genuine sympathy.

'Oh, poor gentleman,' she said, 'it must be.'

'You see,' said Mrs Lorton, 'as a Xtian gentleman he's quite unable to let them go.'

'Oh, quite,' said Parker, 'quite – except for a moment, perhaps, just to get a firmer hold.'

Mrs Lorton opened the door.

'So perhaps you'll help him,' she said, 'all you can.'

Parker glanced at her inquiringly.

'I mean, put his stick under his arm and his hat on.'

'Oh, gladly,' said Parker, 'ever so gladly.'

'And escort him down the drive and open the front gate for him.'

Preceded by Parker, therefore, I left the room, and though it was perhaps unfortunate that there were two other servants in the hall, at Parker's request one of them brought my hat, which Parker herself put on my head, while the other inserted my walking-stick, handle foremost, beneath my left arm-pit. Thanking them graciously, but without undue familiarity, and once again preceded by Parker, I then moved down the drive, of which this gentle domestic opened the front gate for me. Nor was that the last service that she was privileged to render me, for acting upon a suggestion that she had obligingly volunteered, I visited a tailor in Enfield High Street to whom, as I soon discovered, she hoped to be betrothed. An admirable young man, he had not as yet made up his mind as to whether it would be discreet to grant her request, but he was happy to provide me with two entirely new buttons and personally to affix them to the brink of my trousers.

Completely restored, then, in respect of my clothes, and physically recuperated with some excellent buns, I was enabled to assimilate the scenes of my return journey with an even keener appreciation, and to arrive at Paternoster Row in the full confidence of final success. Not having a visiting-card, I had made up my mind to announce myself as a messenger from Mrs Chrysostom; and, as it proved, this was the means of securing me an almost immediate audience. A somewhat short and extremely stout man with a heavily-coloured face and a drooping grey moustache, Mr Chrysostom Lorton, whom I recognized from his photograph, might rather have been a general than a man of commerce; and I cannot say that a first inspection of him gave me entire satisfaction. Undoubtedly well-dressed, with a serpentine gold ring encasing the lower portion of each third finger, I was rather disagreeably affected both by his bushy and protruding eyebrows as well as by his attitude towards a slight mischance associated with the inception of our interview. For in presenting the envelope, with which I had assured him Mrs Chrysostom had entrusted me, I unfortunately in the first place handed him the one in which she had placed my posterior trouser-buttons. For a moment he stared at them with bulging eyeballs, and then I regret to say that he apparently forgot himself.

'Good God,' he said, 'what the hell – crumph, crumph – do you mean, sir?'

Equally surprised, I have always been glad to remember that I was the first to recover my equanimity. Laughing merrily, I handed him the second envelope – in point of bestowal, of course, the first.

'Although you must not assume,' I said, 'that my natural mirth in any degree condones your involuntary blasphemy.'

'Condones my what?' he said. 'Crumph, crumph. But how the devil did she get hold of them?'

Still clinging to the original envelope, whose texture he obviously recognized, his globular eyes continued to be focused on the two buttons before him. Briefly I explained to him the circumstances of their detachment. But for a considerable time he kept referring to the subject.

'I don't like it,' he said, 'I don't like it at all. It's not seemly. It might have been very serious.'

Then a new suspicion darkened his countenance.

'I suppose I may assume,' he said, 'that you've had them replaced?'

I bowed reassuringly.

'By a tailor in Enfield,' I said, 'who was incidentally a great admirer of you.'

His face cleared a little.

'Eh, what?' he said. 'An admirer you say? What was his name?'

I informed him and he nodded his head.

'Ah, yes, yes,' he said, 'a worthy young fellow.'

By an auspicious chance too – if indeed it were one – a female clerk now entered the room, bearing in her hands a specimen copy of the nineteenth edition of the Bible for Schools. He glanced up from his wife's letter.

'Yes, yes,' he said, 'that will interest you.'

'Nothing,' I replied, 'could have interested me more, unless perhaps a specimen of the twentieth.'

Afterwards, as I shall show, my initial distrust of the man proved to have been only too well founded. But, as matters turned out on this particular afternoon, I left his office as a junior assistant. Placed under the charge of the show-room manager, I was to help this gentleman with his accounts and to act when necessary as a salesman of the firm's congenial and Xtian literature. It was a supreme moment – it was perhaps, in a good many ways, the supremest moment of my life – and I did not hesitate, after some further buns, to make suitable acknowledgement of it in St Paul's Cathedral. Nor was the news with which I was confronted on my return to Angela Gardens entirely able to counteract the deep satisfaction with which it filled me.

Nevertheless it was perhaps a timely reminder of the ever-present imminence of eternity, and it was certainly one that I have made a point of recalling in many subsequent moments of elation. For hardly had I opened the front gate when somebody touched me on the shoulder, and turning round, I observed Simeon Whey looking more preoccupied than I had ever seen him. His lips, at any rate, were moving rather convulsively and his laryngeal spasm was extremely marked.

'Kck,' he said. 'It's Silas.'

'Dear me,' I replied. 'What's the matter with him?'

'Kck,' he repeated. 'He's dead.'

'You don't say so?' I cried. 'What did he die of?'

For some seconds he was unable to speak, obviously struggling with his vocal cords, and then with a blast of exceptional sadness he managed to expel the mournful details. Suffering, as it appeared, from a temporary gastric distension, the amiable lad had gone to the medicine chest, where he had unfortunately mistaken the cyanide of potassium for the bicarbonate of soda.

Chapter Ten

*Precautionary measures on entering commercial life. I join the
N.S.L. and the S.P.S.D.T. A crying need in the conduct of
prayer-meetings. I join the A.D.S.U. Personal appearance of
Ezekiel Stool. Personal appearance of his five sisters.
Predicament of Ezekiel Stool on the fifth of November. A timely
instance of presence of mind. I am invited to a meal at the Stools'
residence. A foreshadowing of sinister events.*

It was a distressing end. Few things are more
distressing, indeed, than the sudden demise of a poten-
tial clergyman. And for the first three or four days of
my work in Paternoster Row my spirits were
appreciably clouded. Nevertheless, I was happy not
only that I had embarked upon the career so
satisfactorily chosen for me, but also in the consciousness that, but for my own perspicacity, Providence
would have found it difficult to assist me. Moreover, it
was an additional comfort to me to reflect that, during
my upward progress in the firm, I should have the
obligatory if unwilling support of Mrs Chrysostom
Lorton. A word in the ear of her husband, and her
infamy could be no longer concealed, and I could not
suppose that, callous as she was, she would dare to
expose herself to such an event.

Few young men, therefore, can have entered business
life better equipped or so advantageously placed, and
had I in consequence been carried away a little, it would
scarcely perhaps have been unnatural. Very fortunately,

however, and thanks in a great degree to the character-forming incidents already related, I realized from the outset that I was now definitely committed to the most critical period of a young man's life – namely, the years, so fatal to the vast majority, between his seventeenth and twenty-fourth birthdays. Then it is, alas, that intoxicated with the knowledge that he has become, in my father's phrase, a marriageable adult that he begins to resort for the first time to the tobacconist and the publican – to buy the cigarette that will so inevitably lure him into loose and licentious company, and the fermented liquor that will only too surely encase him in a drunkard's coffin.

Nor is that all. For it is in these same years, turning aside from the pleasures of home – from such innocent round games as Conceal the Thimble or the less familiar Up Jenkins, or from the happy singing round the family harmonium of such a humorous glee as Three Blind Mice – that he enters the Pit (so appropriately named) of some garish and degrading theatre.

It is a sorrowful spectacle. But happily for my own sake, I had already been so deeply saddened by it that I had long since resolved, when the necessity should arise, to take every possible precaution. No sooner, therefore, had I obtained my appointment than I hastened to enrol myself as a member of the Peckham Branch of the Non-Smokers' League as well as of the Kennington Division of the Society for the Prohibition of the Strong Drink Traffic. Congenial in every way, I not only discovered in these an enormous sphere for the exercise of my influence, but the membership of both societies conferred the privilege of wearing a small badge or bone medallion.

A slightly convex and circular plaque to be pinned on the lapel of the wearer's coat, the token of membership of the Non-Smokers' League was about an inch in diameter. Of a pale cream colour, it was tastefully wreathed with dark blue lilies, symbolic of purity, the centre of it being occupied with the initials *N.S.L.* boldly imprinted in the same colours. No less decorative to the wearer than intriguing to the beholder, a reply to the question so often put as to what the initials *N.S.L.* stood for frequently afforded a valuable opportunity for soul-intercourse on the subject of tobacco.

Nor was the medallion of the Society for the Prohibition of the Strong Drink Traffic either less attractive or efficient as an instigator of fruitful converse. Slightly larger – its diameter was an inch and a quarter – its ground-work was of an olive green, the letters *S.P.S.D.T.* richly emerging from this in an ingenious monogram of canary yellow.

Into the work of these societies I now threw myself with all the vehemence at my command, and had soon forced myself into the innermost councils of the local branch of each. Meeting every fortnight in a neighbouring church hall, the Peckham Branch of the Non-Smokers' League did not confine itself merely to the organization of these central gatherings. Valuable as they were in providing a pulpit for lectures upon nicotine poisoning and its attendant evils, we rightly regarded the outside world as the main field of our endeavours. Provided with such strikingly headed pamphlets as *A Gentleman or a Chimney?* or the even more dramatic and spiritually searching *Your Soul or Your Cigar?* we would range the streets addressing obvious smokers, or station ourselves upon the pavement in the neighbourhood of tobacconists' shops. In this way, though frequently required to endure verbal persecution, I am proud to believe that the work performed by us was both timely and enduring.

Working on lines that were somewhat similar, the Kennington Division of the *S.P.S.D.T.* held monthly reunions for the purpose of communally denouncing the use of alcohol; and here we would discuss, over cups of tea and slices of plain but palatable cake, the results of our labours during the previous four weeks and our plans for the four immediately ensuing. Appreciably more dangerous, in that we deemed it our duty to distribute literature at the doors of Public Houses, whence there would emerge in depressingly large numbers combative men of considerable size, we never embarked upon this particular mission save in groups of four or five, each member being provided with a police whistle in addition to his parcel of appropriate leaflets.

Admirably illustrated, these bore such arresting titles as *Passing the Poison* or *From Beer to Bier*, two of the most efficient being *The Dram Drinker's Downfall*, and *Virtue versus Vertigo*. That all these works, like those of the *N.S.L.*, were published by the firm of Chrysostom Lorton was, of course, an additional and pleasurable inducement to further their disposal in every way. And although as yet this could not result for me in any direct financial advantage, it must be remembered that at this time there was still every prospect of its eventually doing so.

To thousands of my readers, slacker in fibre, or not so resolute in the pursuit of goodness, it may well seem now as if these activities must have exhausted my spiritual capacity. But this was not the case, and conscious as I was – it would have been an affectation to deny it – of my very rapidly increasing ability for both religious and commercial leadership, I took every opportunity of developing my unchallenged gift of self-expression. Thus, within a year of my business advent, I had not only addressed both the foregoing societies, but I had become a familiar and, I trust, welcome figure at every local prayer-meeting.

I use the word welcome because I had not only discerned in these gatherings an admirable vehicle of elocutionary progress, but I had quickly discovered in them a crying need that it was plainly my duty to supply. Familiar to every frequenter of the average prayer-meeting, whether Church of England or Non-conformist, this was nothing less than the presence of a gap-filler, especially in the earlier stages of the proceedings. Few can have failed, for example, to notice the pause that almost invariably takes place after the Chairman has delivered his own petition and invited the efforts of further supplicants. Painful in itself, in that it so often accentuates the respiratory difficulties of those present, how often is it broken, alas, by the simultaneous commencement of two or more separate competitors? Nor is that all. For, each realizing that he is too late, a disheartened silence generally ensues, only to be broken perhaps by a second neck-to-neck effort on the part of all the previous starters that abortively collapses again on some such unfortunate phrase as 'Oh dear, oh Lord.'

It was here, then, that I descried, and at once began to work, an almost virgin field, never allowing an instant to elapse after the right to supplicate had been declared general. Indeed on many occasions I filled the subsequent gaps also, and at one particularly reluctant gathering, I can well remember, in less than an hour, offering a dozen full-length petitions. That I soon had rivals goes without saying. Who, in such a position, could have escaped them? But once started, I allowed no second petitioner to deflect or abbreviate my entreaties.

Perhaps the work, however, in which I was most interested was that of the Anti-Dramatic and Saltatory* Union, founded by Ezekiel Stool, the son of Abraham Stool, the inventor and proprietor of Stool's Adult Gripe Water. Probably the most persistent and unflinching opponent that the theatre and dancing saloon have ever known, he was then some twenty-six years of age and of a very remarkable and beautiful character. Indeed all that he lacked of these two qualities in his actual physical appearance seemed to have been concentrated with additional force in his spiritual personality. No taller than myself, and weighing considerably less, he had suffered all his life from an inherent dread of shaving, and the greater portion of his face was in consequence obliterated by a profuse but gentle growth of hair. His voice, too, owing to some developmental defect, had only partially broken; and indeed his father Abraham (afterwards removed to an asylum) had on more than one occasion attempted to sacrifice him, under the mistaken im-

---

* Appertaining to dancing.

100

pression that he was some sort of animal that would be suitable as a burnt offering.

Regarded as a character, however, and when he had fully assured himself that he was not in the presence of a theatre-goer or dancer, it would have been difficult to imagine a more affectionate or deeply trustful companion;* and many an hour we spent together combating the drama, both in Central London and the suburbs. Well provided with money, thanks to the sales of the Gripe Water – an excellent remedy to which I have frequently had recourse – he had himself composed and caused to be printed several extremely powerful leaflets. Of these perhaps the best were *The Chorus Girl's Catastrophe* and *Did Wycliffe Waltz?* and these we would distribute in large numbers among the degenerate pleasure-seekers standing outside theatres. Purchasing seats, too, we would ourselves from time to time enter these buildings, rising in our places when the curtain was drawn up and audibly rebuking the performers. Needless to say, having registered our protest, we would then immediately leave the premises, not always immune from the coarse objurgations of obviously interested minions.

Nor were we less vigorous in our onslaught upon the equally prevalent sin of dancing, either personally attending or stationing delegates at the entrances to halls or private houses, and endeavouring if possible by individual appeals to warn or deter would-be malefactors. An uphill task, it was not for us to say to how great an extent we may have succeeded, but I can remember at least twelve persons, male and female, who

* It was far otherwise, alas, in later years.

promised to consider what we had pointed out to them.

Deeply as I appreciated, however, the opportunity of furthering this valuable and congenial work, I had not as yet realized the ultimate object that an inscrutable Providence had in view, or that in Ezekiel Stool I had already been handed the compass that was destined to lead my steps to matrimony. Such was the case, however, little as I then dreamed it, and even less, if such a thing were possible, was I attracted, on a first acquaintance, to any of his five sisters. Simply divided into twins and triplets, these were all younger than Ezekiel himself, the triplets being then twenty-four, and the twins three years younger. None of them was married, and indeed, as regarded the triplets, this was scarcely perhaps to be wondered at. For though they had been interestingly named by their father as Faith, Hope, and Charity, they were plain girls, deeply marked by smallpox, and of rather less than the average intelligence. Nor indeed were the twins, Tact and Understanding, at all remarkable for personal beauty, and the toes of one of them, as I was afterwards to discover, were most unfortunately webbed. On the other hand, they were kindly, domestic creatures. All five of them could play the piano. And the heart of each, as they have frequently told me, was profoundly stirred by my first visit.

Little as I shared, however, though I could not fail to perceive, the cardiac exaltation of these five females, I have always looked back to that first visit with a very considerable degree of pleasure, and not the less so because of the preliminary service that I was able to render their brother Ezekiel. Indeed it was this that led to an invitation to share the evening meal at the Stools' house, a substantial residence with a large garden, about five minutes' walk from Camberwell Green.

A November dusk, some eighteen months or so after my entrance into commercial life, I had forgotten that it was the anniversary of the attempt of Guy Fawkes to destroy the Upper Chamber of our Legislature, and my thoughts were engaged upon other matters as I began to walk home from the omnibus stopping-place. I had hardly walked a hundred yards, however, when my attention was suddenly attracted to a somewhat vociferous group of boys, in the midst of whom, to my surprise and anxiety, I saw my friend Ezekiel Stool. For a moment I was at a loss both as how to proceed and the possible reason for the conclave. But a moment later I discovered that the position was no less disturbing than grotesque. Doubtless intoxicated with the memories of the day, these ignorant and turbulent youths had apparently discerned in my friend Ezekiel a resemblance to the conspirator of 1605. Nay, they had gone further. They had professed to perceive in him an actual reincarnation of the original miscreant, and this in spite of the fact that Ezekiel had repeatedly explained to them that he had no knowledge of pyrotechnics.

'Believe me,' he had said, 'I am neither the man you mention, nor do I resemble any authentic portrait of him. Nor have I placed explosives under anybody's chamber either in London or the Provinces.'

Despite his denials, however, supported as they were by references to prominent local residents, the group of vociferators was quickly growing both in numbers and excitement, and several suggestions were being audibly

103

made that he should be exterminated by fire. It was a moment for action, and I took it. Fortunately my police whistle was in my pocket. And in the next instant I was blowing blast upon blast to the utmost capacity of my lung power. The effect was immediate. For scarcely had the boys dispersed when three or four constables arrived on the scene, all of them breathless from the act of running, but carrying their truncheons in their hands. Being breathless too, I could only point at Ezekiel, and for the first moment they misunderstood me, rapidly surrounding him, as he leaned against a lamp-post, and lifting their truncheons above their heads. Once again, therefore, it was a moment for action, and once again I took it. Throwing myself in front of him, I shouted to them to forbear, and then very briefly I explained what had happened. Unfortunately, as I have said, the boys had already dispersed. But then, as I pointed out to them, that had been my object, and the fact that this had taken place before their arrival was no reflection upon their courage. I cannot record, however, that their reception of this news was either Xtian or even courteous, and it was a very great relief both to myself and Ezekiel when these powerful professionals at last went away. Nevertheless, as Ezekiel said, I had probably twice saved his life, and during the evening meal, to which he at once invited me, both his parents and his five sisters repeatedly expressed their satisfaction. Mr Abraham Stool, indeed, who had not then been segregated, but who was already under the impression that he was the Hebrew patriarch, several times insisted upon my approaching him and placing my hand under his left thigh, after which he would offer me, in addition to Mrs Stool, a varying number of rams and goats.

Needless to say, I declined to accept these, and a week or two later, as I have already indicated, it was deemed advisable, owing to his tendency to sacrifice, to place him in other and remoter surroundings. But it was a happy evening, during which, as I shall always remember, Ezekiel Stool expressed his regret that my father and myself were not fellow-worshippers with them at St Nicholas, Newington Butts. Satisfied as we were, however, with St James-the-Least-of-All, where my father had now become senior sidesman, we had seen no reason, as I was obliged to point out to him, for again transferring our worship; and little did I dream that even as I was speaking those sinister events were already shaping themselves that were ultimately to unite us – their only redeeming outcome – in this new and closer bond.

Chapter Eleven

Design for my grandfather's tomb. Death and interment of Mrs
Emily Smith and the aunt that had stood with my mother's
mother at the bottom of the stairs. Effect upon my father's health.
Alexander Carkeek and his sons. Arrival home from the Stools.
First tidings of the new lectern. My father's interview with the
vicar. Curious instance of transposition of consonants. My
father rehearses his denunciation. Arrival of Simeon Whey.
My father repeats his denunciation.

Permanently impaired as had been my father's health
by the ordeal referred to in Chapter Eight he had not
permitted this, as I have said, to interfere with his
duties as a sidesman; and there were still occasions
upon which he would exhibit all his old-time fire and
determination. Thus when my mother's parents had
been destroyed by a tram accident about a month after
the decease of Silas Whey, it was he who had arranged
the funeral, chosen the hymns, and designed the
monument by which they were to be commemorated.
The provision business having declined somewhat, the
chief factor in the design had necessarily been one of
economy, and my father had therefore confined himself
to a broken column some three inches in diameter and a
foot high. Insufficient to accommodate their full names,
their initials had been tastefully engraved upon it, the
surface of the grave being sprinkled with flints that
would require no subsequent upkeep.

In conjunction with Mr Balfour Whey, too, it was he
who had selected a house for my mother's eight sisters,

small but sufficient and in a remote part of Wales, where they would be able to husband their meagre income. Bitterly opposed as the eight sisters had been both to living together and leaving Walworth, my father had overcome them by the sheer power of his torrential eloquence and personality. Surrounded by strangers, as he had irresistibly reminded them, most of whom were unacquainted with the English language, fifteen miles from a railway station and three and a half from the nearest village, they would have neither the occasion nor the opportunity to dissipate their substance in convivial extravagance, while the precipitous roads, by which alone the house that he had chosen for them could be approached, would give them an appetite for the extremely simple fare which would be all that their means would allow them to purchase. To Wales they had gone, therefore, and though he continued to receive letters from them, couched in terms of the basest ingratitude, he neither replied to these nor permitted them to modify his kindly consideration for my mother.

Nor had he been less adequate in dealing with the circumstances that had arisen, a few months later, in connection with the demises of Mrs Emily Smith and the aunt that had stood with my mother's mother at the foot of the stairs. Both these ladies, who had been living on Post Office annuities, had unhappily died after sharing a sausage, strongly suspected, though never actually proved, of harbouring the bacillus of botulism. Thanks to my father's efforts, however, seconded by Mr Balfour Whey, the firm by whom the sausage had been manufactured consented without prejudice to pay a sum of money sufficient to provide for the ladies'

From a portrait of the Aunt who stood with my mother's mother at the foot of the stairs

interment. I have said sufficient, but after my father had reimbursed himself and paid the expenses of Mr Whey, he was once more faced, as in the case of my grandparents, with an acute necessity for economy. Burying them in a double coffin, however, of his own design – a design for which he afterwards obtained the patent – he succeeded not only in keeping the undertaker's bill within the balance at his disposal, but in providing a surplus with which he afterwards obtained a small iron slab containing their names and ages. Nor was that all, for with the pound or two that was over he bought a third-class ticket to Aberdeen, where he had obtained a situation for Mrs Emily Smith's granddaughter as housemaid in a home for Xtian workers.

After every such exhibition of pristine vigour, however, my father experienced an acute reaction, and for many weeks would become a martyr not only to neurasthenic indigestion, but to digestive neurasthenia accompanied by flatulence of the severest order. For months on end, indeed, my mother would be obliged to sit by his bedside in case he should wake up and require abdominal kneading, and few were the nights upon which she had not in addition to go downstairs and make him some cocoa. But he would never allow himself to be daunted. His breakfast the next morning would be as hearty as usual. And he was never deterred by even the most obstinate inflation from the performance of a moral or religious duty. Despite his courage, however, he was leaning on me with ever-increasing emphasis, and I am proud to recall that, in what was so soon to prove the heaviest ordeal of his life,

I was able to render him very material and indeed essential assistance.

Such, then, was the position when I parted with the Stools, after the evening meal that I have just recorded. And it was rather with their cries of thanks and gentle admiration resounding through the chill November night than with any sense of impending trouble that I turned my footsteps towards home. Indeed, as I buttoned up my overcoat and drew my scarf over my mouth, I had every reason to feel content both on my own account and my father's, whose health for some weeks had been slowly improving. For not only had my mother's parents been safely interred and her eight sisters satisfactorily disposed of, her two aunts competently buried, and Emily Smith junior despatched to Aberdeen, but my father, as I have indicated, had finally established himself as the senior sidesman of St James-the-Least-of-All.

Conferring the right of leading the other sidesmen up the central aisle at the end of the collection, this was the more gratifying since my father had only obtained it as the result of a prolonged and determined struggle, in which his chief opponent had been a retired fish-monger, known as Alexander Carkeek. A northern Caledonian of the most offensive type, this gentleman, as he liked to consider himself, was now a sleeping partner in the firm of Carkeek and Carkeek, fishmongers and poulterers in the Kennington Road, and had long been suspected, both by my father and myself, of a secret addiction to alcohol. Of middle height – he was perhaps taller than my father by an inch and three-quarters or two inches – his abdominal circumference was equally extensive and his bullet-shaped face even more highly coloured. Unlike my father, however, he had signally failed in retaining the bulk of his hair, and even his two sons, Corkran and Cosmo, were showing signs of becoming bald. Sidesmen like their father, they were only less aggressive, and during the long contest for supremacy, they had seized every opportunity of detaining or distracting my father while their own got into position at the head of the line. Indeed on one occasion, when my father had paused for a moment to adjust a door-handle half-way up the aisle, they had deliberately encouraged their father to push himself in front and thereby head the procession. Naturally resenting this, my father had immediately plunged forward, with the painful result that the two of them had become wedged and had been unable, owing to their respective girths, either to advance or retreat. Needless to say, in the struggle that ensued, my father had been the first to break away and had arrived at the chancel half an abdomen ahead of his pertinacious rival.

Ultimately, as I have said, however, thanks to repeated protests and an impassioned interview with the vicar, my father had definitely secured for himself the right of precedence, though the Carkeeks still remained sidesmen. Nor was that all. For it was now generally known that the vicar's churchwarden was about to retire, and there could be little doubt, as my father had several times observed to me, as to the probable successor to this great position.

It was with a comparatively light heart, therefore, that I opened the front door, hung up my hat and coat and folded my scarf, and entered the parlour ready to describe to my father the events that had occupied my evening; and my distress can be imagined when I at once perceived him to be in a state of the acutest physical congestion. Facially suffused to an alarming extent, the hairs of his moustache were visibly projecting, and I naturally assumed at first that he must have become the subject of an exceptional degree of intestinal discomfort. On closer inspection, however, I observed that this could scarcely be the case since his waistcoat buttons were still fastened, and for a brief second I had a fearful apprehension that he was annoyed with myself. He did, in fact, ask me rather abruptly the reason for my absence from the evening meal. But his expression lightened a little when I told him where I had been and of the services rendered by me to Ezekiel Stool.

'Yes, it's a good family,' he said, 'a very good family, and there's money in it as well as religion.'

The next moment, however, his face had resumed its congestion, and as I leaned back while my mother unlaced my boots, it became increasingly evident to me that I was in the presence of a spiritual crisis of the gravest kind. Nay, even then, I remember, I had a sudden presentiment that here was a situation of no common significance, and I signalled to my mother to be as rapid as possible in bringing me my slippers and leaving us alone. Then I took a deep breath and, leaning forward a little, gently touched my father's knee.

'Can I not help you?' I said.

My father stared at me. For perhaps a minute his lips moved convulsively. Then in a strangled voice he uttered a single word, followed a little later by fourteen other words.

113

'Carkeek,' he said. 'It's that fellow Carkeek. He's been and presented the church with a lectern.'

For a moment I was utterly dumbfounded.

'A lectern?' I asked.

My father nodded. 'Made of brass,' he said, 'in the image of a bird.'

'Of a bird?' I cried. 'What sort of bird?'

'Of an eagle,' said my father, 'looking towards the left.'

'Towards the left?' I said. 'But where's it to stand?'

'At the top of the aisle,' said my father, 'just below the chancel steps.'

'But, dear father,' I cried, 'we already have a lectern,' and indeed this was literally the case, since the cavity or enclosure adjoining the choir seats, from which the vicar or his curate read the service, was also provided with a separate book-rest for the purpose of delivering the lessons.

'Yes, I know,' said my father, 'but that wouldn't deter Carkeek.'

'But surely,' I cried, 'the vicar hasn't accepted it?'

'He has not only accepted it,' said my father, 'but the thing's in position.'

'In position,' I said, 'and looking to the left?'

My father nodded again.

'Just west of south,' he said.

'But good heavens,' I cried, 'I say it in all reverence, then it must be staring right into our pew.'

'So it is,' said my father, 'and not only that, the brazen hell-bird's protruding its tongue.'

The room darkened a little.

'But not intentionally?' I asked. 'You don't mean to

say that it's protruding its tongue intentionally?'

My father gulped once or twice. Then he bowed his head.

'Yes, I do,' he said, 'and I say it deliberately.'

Then he rose to his feet and stood looking down at me.

'And that's not the worst,' he said, 'not by a long way.'

'Not the worst?' I cried. 'What do you mean?'

My father swayed a little, but managed to recover himself.

'I mean this,' he said. 'I mean that Alexander Carkeek is trying to get himself made churchwarden.'

For a moment I was stunned. My father sat heavily down again.

'But good God,' I cried, 'that amounts to simony.'

'I know,' said my father. 'That's what I've told Carkeek.'

'Then you've seen him?' I said.

My father looked at me grimly.

'I've not only seen him,' he answered, 'but I've told him what I thought of him. And I've explicitly informed him that if he's made a churchwarden, I shall take proceedings against him in the ecclesiastical courts.'

My father leaned back closing his eyes, and I had never admired him more, perhaps, than at that moment.

'And the vicar,' I said. 'Have you spoken to the vicar?'

'I was obliged to warn him,' said my father, 'in identical terms.'

'You could do no less,' I said. 'But what about the bird itself?'

'I regret to say,' said my father, 'that he professed to

admire it.'

I stared at him aghast.

'Professed to admire it?' I gasped. 'The vicar that we have supported all these years?'

My father covered his eyes for a moment.

'Even so,' he said. 'As I had to point out to him, I was seriously shaken.'

'But surely you protested,' I cried.

'For seventy-five minutes,' said my father.

'But couldn't he perceive,' I said, 'that it was a direct insult to us?'

My father moved his hand a little.

'He claimed that it was not so. He said that the majority of these birds looked towards the left.'

'But not with their tongues out,' I cried.

'He seemed to think so. He said it was symbolic of inward joy.'

'But good heavens,' I said, 'I repeat it with all reverence, does he expect us to worship under conditions like that?'

'I'm sorry to say,' said my father, 'that he had appeared to contemplate it prior to my insistence on its immediate removal.'

My heart gave a great leap.

'Then it's being taken down?' I cried.

But my father stared at me with bulging eyes. My heart fell back again.

'I don't know,' he said. 'That's why I'm preparing my denunciation.'

It was a solemn moment. It was perhaps the solemnest moment that either of us had been called upon to experience, and even as I spoke, I felt that we were drawing towards the threshold of one of the greatest issues of our terrestrial life.

'Then he refused?' I said.

'Let me be quite fair,' said my father. 'He rather temporized than actually refused.'

I could not help smiling a little sardonically.

'The distinction is a fine one,' I said. 'I suppose he adduced some grounds?'

My father breathed heavily.

'He was insolent enough to remind me,' he said, 'that it was eight o'clock on Saturday evening and that the bird in question, which had only just been set up, weighed approximately a quarter of a ton. He also suggested that the congregation ought to have an opportunity of inspecting it.'

'The congregation?' I cried. 'But what has the congregation to do with it? It's not putting its tongue out at the congregation.'

My father inclined his head.

'Precisely what I told him,' he said, 'but he merely fell back upon his previous argument, that the exposure of the tongue, if indeed it were a tongue, was merely significant of good tidings.'

'I see,' I said. 'So you gave him an ultimatum?'

'I was compelled to,' said my father. 'There was no other course. Either it must be removed, I told him, before tomorrow morning or I should publicly denounce it during morning service.'

'And what did he say?' I asked.

My father made a contemptuous gesture.

'Oh, you know what he is,' he replied, 'a weed before the rind.'

'You mean a reed,' I said.

'What did I say?' said my father.

'You said a weed,' I said.

'I said a weed?' said my father.

'A weed before the wind,' I said. 'I mean the rind.'

'The rind?' said my father. 'But that's wrong.'

'Yes. But that's what you said,' I said.

'A weed before the rind?' said my father.

'Yes, a transposition,' I explained, 'of the initial consonants.'

'A transposition?' inquired my father.

'Yes, an error in enunciation,' I said, 'such as frequently takes place under emotional stress.'

'But, I don't understand,' said my father.

'You meant a reed before the wind,' I said.

'Well, of course,' said my father. 'That's what I said.'

'No, you said a weed,' I said, 'a weed before the rind.'

'But how can a weed be before the rind?' said my father.

'But you didn't mean that,' I said. 'You meant a reed before the wind.'

'Well, that's what he is,' said my father. 'That's just what I say. That's why he implored me not to make a denunciation.'

'But of course you will,' I said.

My father nodded.

'Immediately after the collection,' said my father, 'and before the blessing.'

I looked at the clock. It was a quarter past ten. In an hour and three-quarters the Sabbath would be upon us. There was not much time. I glanced at my father anxiously.

'How far have you got?' I asked.

'About half-way,' he said.

Then he rose to his feet again and crossed to the harmonium.

'Ring for the cocoa,' he said. I sprang to the bell. But just as I reached it my mother entered, bearing two cups of the sustaining fluid. Signalling to her to withdraw, he lifted one of the cups and drained its contents at a single gulp.

'Now, listen,' he said, and in a low but rising voice, he began a denunciation that I shall never forget.

Impeccable in logic, succinct in argument, perfect in phrasing and faultlessly delivered, I have never, I think, listened to so moving an utterance as the initial moiety of my father's denunciation. Beginning, as I have said, in a low voice, yet one that was crystal clear in its penetrating capacity, for the first five minutes or so my father refused to allow himself the adventitious aid of a single gesture. It was the gathering of the storm, as it were, the marshalling of the hosts of heaven, composed but relentless, above the brazen image. Then he paused for a moment, indicating the aspidistra that stood upon a tripod in the corner of the room.

'Now, say that's the bird,' he said, and suddenly, like a flash of lightning, his right index finger was quivering upon the air. Involuntarily I leapt round and stared at the aspidistra, and then like the deafening down-burst of a tornado, my father expanded his chest, threw back his head, and opened the full flood-gates of his passion. Pallid and cowering, I crept behind the armchair, while syllable after syllable rent the night, and the delirious harmonium leapt and crashed down again beneath the

119

palpitant thunder of his blows. Then almost as suddenly he stopped.

'That's as far as I've got,' he said.

I crept from my shelter.

'Is there to be much more?' I asked.

'About five minutes' calm,' he said, 'and then the final, culminating climax.'

He wiped his forehead.

'I've got it roughed out,' he said, 'if you'd like to hear it before it's rounded off.'

I signified my assent, and he proceeded. But indeed it already seemed to me to be practically flawless, while the ultimate crescendo, prepared as I had believed myself, left me literally prostrate and fighting for breath. My father, on the other hand, although he was perspiring freely, seemed to have become endowed with a new lease of life, and was able single-handed to replace the harmonium which had fallen upon its face during his closing sentence. Then there came a low knock on the parlour window. It was nearly eleven; we stared at each other startled; and it was with considerable relief that we perceived the newcomer to be no more important than Simeon Whey. Yet his errand was a kind one, although it was a considerable time before he was sufficiently master of himself to explain his presence, while we had already foreseen and prepared for the tidings that had brought the admirable youth to our window.

Hearing from his father, whom my father had already consulted, of the very great trouble with which we were threatened, he had put on his hat and coat, wrapped his scarf round his neck, and immediately hurried to St

James-the-Least-of-All. There, with infinite cunning and hardly less devotion, he had managed to conceal himself behind a tombstone, where he had awaited for nearly an hour and a half the arrival of workmen to remove the lectern. None had come, however, and somewhere about half-past ten, he had reluctantly abandoned his vigil and, faint with hunger, hurried to Angela Gardens to apprise us of its result.

'Kck,' he said, when we had given him a biscuit, 'I'm afraid it'll be a case of denunciation.'

My father nodded grimly.

'So I had anticipated,' he said. 'In fact, I had just been denouncing when you knocked at the window.'

'Kck,' said Simeon – now a theological student – 'I should like to have heard you.'

My father glanced at me, and I inclined my head.

'I'll do it again,' he said, and he returned to the harmonium.

Nor was he less powerful than on the first occasion, and I shall never forget his effect on Simeon Whey. Beginning as before in a low voice, yet one that was crystal clear in its penetrative capacity, for the first five minutes or so he refused to allow himself the adventitious aid of a single gesture. It was the gathering of the storm, as it were, the marshalling of the hosts of heaven, composed but relentless, above the brazen image. Then he paused for a moment, again indicating the aspidistra that stood upon a tripod in the corner of the room.

'Now, say that's the bird,' he said, and suddenly, like a flash of lightning, his right index finger was quivering upon the air. Involuntarily Simeon leapt round and stared at the aspidistra, and then like the deafening down-burst of a tornado, my father expanded his chest, threw back his head, and opened the full flood-gates of his passion. Pallid and cowering, Simeon crept behind the armchair while syllable after syllable rent the night, and the delirious harmonium leapt and crashed down again beneath the palpitant thunder of my father's blows. Then for five minutes there was a comparative calm, while Simeon Whey crept from his shelter, until the ultimate crescendo stretched him helpless on the carpet, blue in the face, and fighting for his breath. Then he staggered to his feet and sank into the armchair, while my father once more picked up the harmonium.

'Oh, kck,' he said, 'kck.'

It was all that the poor youth was able to utter.

Chapter Twelve

Breakfast finds us calm but grave. My mother is allowed to
accompany us to church. My father's clothing and general
demeanour. Remark of Simeon Whey on my father's hat. First
impression of the new lectern. Unmistakable evidences of guilt.
The vicar's feeble apologia. A devilish device and its disastrous
results. I race with Corkran for half-a-crown. My poor father is
three times dropped.

Impeccable in logic, as I have already said, succinct in
argument, and perfect in phrasing, it is with the
profoundest regret that I have been obliged to omit
from these pages the actual words of my father's
denunciation; and I should like to make it quite clear
that for the inevitable disappointment my publishers
alone must bear the blame. Bitterly as I have protested,
however, they have replied to every argument with
sordid references to the cost of production, and this
volume has in consequence been rushed through the
press deprived of my poor father's terrible indictment.*
Nor is this the less deplorable because at the last
moment my father himself was prohibited from
uttering it, owing to an intervention of Providence as
little to have been expected as it has always appeared to
me inexplicable. Indeed, had we foreseen it, I doubt if

* It is my full intention, however, to pursue this matter further,
and any reader desirous of signing an appeal should instantly
communicate with me at Wilhelmina, Nassington Park Gardens,
Hornsey.

either my father or myself would have been able to retain his sanity, and we should certainly not have met, as we did the next morning, in a comparatively cheerful frame of mind.

Yet this was the case, and although, as each of us remarked, the expression of the other was unwontedly grave, it was a relief to us both to learn that neither of us had spent a bad, or even indifferent, night. Considering the circumstances, indeed, we had slept remarkably well, and in view of the tremendous task that now certainly awaited us, each of us was scrupulous to fortify his person with as large and nourishing a meal as possible. As we sang the morning hymn, too, I was glad to perceive that my father's voice was in exceptional condition, while the sunshine and soft air augured well for a particularly large congregation.

'The more, the better,' said my father, and he even went so far as to permit the attendance of my mother, thereby excusing her from her usual task of preparing our midday meal or dinner.

'We'll have something cold,' he said, 'middle day, and she shall give us a good hot meal after evening service.'

With myself on his right, then, and my mother on his left, we left the house at 10.45, and I have never, I think, seen my father so meticulously dressed as on this stern but necessary occasion. Wearing his longest frock-coat, a double-breasted gentian waistcoat, faultlessly creased trousers, and the glossiest of brown boots, his collar was encircled with a cream-coloured velvet tie, held in position by a single Cape garnet. By a happy circumstance, too, his bowler hat had only been purchased the week before; and indeed, as Simeon whispered to me, it might rather have been that of some French aristocrat mounting the tumbril than of a Xtian sidesman of the United Kingdom on his way to denounce a lectern. Nor did he hesitate to lift it when we met Mr and Mrs Carkeek, accompanied by Cosmo and Corkran, although I have seen nothing more distant than the inclination of the head with which he signified consciousness of their presence. As Simeon said to me: 'Your father may be a Xtian, but he never forgets that he's a gentleman.'

We were now on the brink, however, of the church porch – a couple of steps and the effigy would be in sight – and deeply as we had impressed upon each other the necessity for self-command, I could not help staggering a little and leaning against Simeon. My father staggered too, leaning against Mr Balfour Whey, while my mother staggered against Mrs Meatson, the obliging wife of Mr Meatson, the editor of the parish magazine. Then with a supreme effort we recovered our equilibria, and in the next moment — albeit at a distance – we were facing an image that, for malignant effrontery, was surely unparalleled in Church history.

I say facing, for although its actual countenance was turned, as I have said, towards the left, its malevolent bosom as well as its right eye were directly focussed upon our persons. Nor can I trust myself, even now, to describe its effect upon us as we moved up the aisle, although every detail of its repulsive appearance was indelibly graved upon my memory. Suffice it to say, therefore, that it gave the general impression of a vulture rather than an eagle; that it appeared to have robbed an arsenal of a medium-sized cannon-ball, upon

125

Alexander Parkeek and his two sons

which it now stood poised on the summit of a mast; and that its outspread wings had been blasphemously converted into a support for the Holy Scriptures. Nor was that all, for at each corner of the pedestal, in which the mast had been embedded, was an additional claw with projecting talons of undisguised ferocity – the total effect from the bottom of the aisle being that of a six-clawed monster about to expectorate.

Repellent as was its appearance, however, even at a distance, it was not until we drew nearer to it up the central aisle that I suddenly became aware in it of a quite unforeseen and infinitely sinister significance. For now, as we approached our pew, which was the front one on the right, it was perfectly clear that its eyes had been so fashioned as to be capable of regarding us, either separately or in unison, with an almost un-believable degree of venom. But they could do more, for what was my horror, just as we were about to turn into our pew, to perceive that my father, whose colour had visibly deepened, was still holding on towards the chancel. Nay, to be exact, he was still holding on towards the very image that he had come to condemn, with his two eyes fixed and slowly converging upon the baleful eye-ball of the bird itself. For a moment I stood spellbound. What was he about to do? And then, as the pew rocked beneath my feet, I suddenly realized that my poor father had been foully and deliberately hypnotized.

It was a critical instant. Another couple of steps, and one of two things must inevitably have happened. He would either have dashed his forehead against the bird's bosom, or his abdomen would have collided with the mast. Nor was the danger less real because it was as yet unperceived either by my mother or the rest of the congregation. With an enormous effort, however, I succeeded in rallying myself and, seizing and compressing my father's right elbow, steering him half-conscious into his usual place, where he immediately fell forward upon his knees. Then I bent down. 'It was the bird's eye,' I said. 'Whatever you do, avoid the bird's eye,' and ample was my reward in the immensely powerful squeeze which was the only thanks he was able to bestow.

But the danger was not over, for, now that we were in our pew, we were being permanently impinged upon by the bird's full visage, and I saw at once that we should be taxed to the uttermost to sustain its gaze until the end of the service. Regarded from this aspect, however, in which its competing tongue masked the malignity of its eyes, its expression was less menacing than insolent, albeit to an almost intolerable extent. And it was obviously in the exposed eye, solitary and unchallenged, with which it had followed us up the aisle, that its concentrated malice had found the weapon most effective for its purpose. Temporarily released, therefore, from the acutest personal anxiety, I was at last in a position to observe my fellow-worshippers, and I would that I could record even some semblance of resentment at the loathsome object with which they had been confronted. Upon no face, however, could I see anything inscribed beyond an unintelligent curiosity, while upon many I could not fail to observe an even more lamentable admiration.

Indeed I could hear actual whispers, indicative of approval, such as 'Did you ever, now?' or 'Isn't it handsome?' while some put such queries to one another as: 'What do you suppose it cost?' 'Whoever could have paid for it?' and 'Hasn't it got a polish?' Nor have I seen anything, I think, quite so nauseating to a sensitive Xtian stomach as the scarcely-concealed triumph so smugly discernible upon the faces of the four Carkeeks. My only reassurance, in fact, lay in the reflection that my father's denunciation had yet to come; that in so large an assembly there must surely be one or two to whom the bird's true character must have been obvious; and that the vicar and his curate, who were now nervously entering, had not finally committed themselves. Then the organ ceased playing, the vicar, who was plucking at his surplice, hastily glanced at my father, and the curate, whom I had never seen paler, tremblingly embarked upon the service.

Pale as was the curate, however, and staccato as was the utterance, he was the very embodiment of self-confidence compared with the vicar when the latter first approached the lectern under the steadfast gaze of my dear father; and I have seldom seen the consciousness of guilt take such visible toll of an alleged Xtian clergyman as when this weak prelate staggered from his corner and clung tottering to Carkeek's eagle. Nor had I perceived until then – or not so fully – the profound wisdom that had been my father's in concealing from these men the exact moment at which he intended to make his protest. For they were thus proceeding in the devastating knowledge that at any syllable they might be cut short, and publicly arraigned before the whole congregation for their base act of betrayal.

In spite of my anxiety, therefore, I could scarcely

suppress a smile, and I was glad to observe, as I glanced at my father, that he was once more in complete command both of himself and the situation. Indeed I had never heard him in such stupendous voice as during the hymn that preceded the sermon, and it was obvious that the vicar conceived this to be the prelude to the actual deliverance of the indictment. It was at any rate some moments before he was able to speak, and I have never, I think, heard a more pitiable noise than the quavering tones in which he uttered the words of Jeremiah: 'Mine heritage is unto me as a speckled bird.' *

Spoken by the prophet, he said, under conditions of considerable stress – and who had known more stress than the prophet Jeremiah? – it might also be rendered, as the margin so beautifully reminded us, as a bird having talons. Mine heritage is unto me as a bird having talons – here he paused for a moment, avoiding my father's eye – or might he not say, perhaps, using the plural, *our* heritage is a bird having talons? For in this great gift, this unique gift, that few of us could have failed, he thought, to have noticed, we were all participators, even the most degraded of us, thanks to the generosity of Mr Carkeek. Yes, it was indeed *our* heritage, *ours*, a speckled bird, a bird having talons. And who could say that the care-stricken prophet had not foreseen this beautiful lectern?

For it was a beautiful lectern — few, he thought, could deny this – this speckled bird, this bird having talons. And yet it might well be that, owing to its very unexpectedness, it should give rise to differing opinions. Nay, he would go further. He would hope that it might, for they were all there, he trowed, in a double

*Jeremiah xii. 9.

capacity – as human beings, overflowing with gratitude, but also as trustees for the church's furniture.

Yes, they were trustees. They must never forget that. That was a distinction that he would have them remember. They were not only human beings, but they were churchmen and trustees – church-beings, trustees and human men – yea, and women also, churchees and trust-men; furniture-women, church-trusts and humanees. They were all those things, and they would remember the old saying, so many men, so many opinions. Thus it might be argued – and very reasonably argued – that the present reading-desk was sufficient, and that the very magnificence of this noble bird might a little detract from its holy purpose. As for that, the congregation must judge. He would welcome the opinion of each one of them. There was not one of them whose opinion he would not welcome, even the lowliest and most sinful. For though our heritage had come unto us as a speckled bird, as a bird having talons, it did not necessarily follow that it was our Xtian duty to take it up and enter into it. Many great men, as they were doubtless aware, had given up heritages of considerable value, and who should say that they had not been actuated by the highest and most holy considerations? But others like Esau had lived to regret it. It was a matter for the congregation to decide, united though they would be in their undying appreciation of the splendid munificence of Mr Carkeek. A speckled bird, a bird having talons – let them not lightly discard their heritage. But let them not, on the other hand, too lightly accept it as a bird of no moment. Then, with obvious relief, and indeed a certain amount of complacence, he hurriedly backed down the pulpit steps, just as the curate, leaping to his feet, gave out the number of the closing hymn.

But my father was not perturbed. Throughout the whole service, indeed, he had sat there expressionless as a sphinx, but none the less terrible, because his unwinking eyes had given no hint of their ultimate purpose. Then he rose to his feet, carrying his offertory plate, and it was only in the very deliberateness with which he did so that the most discerning might have gathered a hint, perhaps, of the stupendous judgement about to fall from him. Nor did he allow the task, which was now so imminent, to interfere with his usual custom of joining in the hymn to his uttermost capacity as he moved from pew to pew collecting the offertory.

But the great moment was now close at hand, and I could not forbear turning for a moment in my place and glancing down the aisle at the procession of sidesmen, already formed and waiting my father's signal. For from now onwards even I myself was a little uncertain of my father's intentions, although I did not apprehend that he would begin his denunciation before the last of the sidesmen had yielded up his plate. Then I glanced at the vicar, who had come to the chancel steps; at the curate, who was plucking at his stole; and finally at the bird, with its brazen eye fixed as before on my approaching father. For the hymn had come to an end now and the procession was in motion, with my father in the van carrying his plate, followed by Alexander Carkeek, Mr Balfour Whey, Mr Meatson, Cosmo and Corkran. Slowly they proceeded, with Mr Carkeek, as usual, chafing at the necessity of having to march second, but obviously intoxicated with pride and self-satisfaction as the people in the pews craned their heads to look at him. So disgusting indeed did I find the spectacle that I was obliged for some seconds to close my eyes, and it was during this brief interval that there happened the awful thing that was finally to shatter my father's health. For when I opened them again, pale and petrified, it was once more to behold my father caught and transfixed and stertorously advancing into the same ingenious and devilish trap.

But now it was too late, though I gave a great cry, and yet that cry, perhaps, may have modified the disaster. For at the last instant, as though he had half-regained consciousness, my father swerved a little to the right, albeit only to stumble and fall at full length over the south-west talons of the pedestal. And yet even then the sidesman in him remained uppermost. For though a half-crown had been jerked from his plate, he never let this go until he had safely grounded it at the very feet of the vicar. Nay, he rose higher. For observing that the half-crown was hurrying towards a grating at the end of the transept, and perceiving that Corkran Carkeek, obeying his family's instinct, had suddenly leapt forward and was hastening after it, he bade me try and secure it before the young Caledonian had succeeded in capturing it for his own box.

'But your poor self?' I cried.

'Never mind me,' he said, 'or he'll get his foot on that half-crown.'

And it was then, and only then, that he yielded to Nature with shriek after shriek of unutterable pain.

It was an astounding moment. For there were thus

two spectacles competing for the attention of the congregation, most of whom had now risen and were standing on their seats in the natural desire to observe events. For in the first place there was my father, writhing on his abdomen at the foot of the lectern, and in the second there were Corkran and myself engaged in the bitterest of races to save and recapture the half-crown. Nor did I win. For though I managed to overtake him, he got his boot upon it at the last moment, just as I had stooped and was about to lift it up at the very brink of the grating. Choking as I was, however, and in spite of his exceptional height, I was able to look him full in the collar and assure him that from that moment I should cease to number him amongst even the most distant of my acquaintances. Then, dumb with wrath and blinded with tears, I managed to swing round upon my heels as the remaining sidesmen, assisted by the vicar and curate, succeeded in raising my poor father.

But the ordeal was not over. Nay, it had hardly begun. For not only did they drop him in the south transept, but they dropped him a second time in the side aisle, and again upon the threshold of the vestry. Whether this was intentional will never be known, or not until that Day when all shall be made clear. But I cannot help mentioning that the Carkeeks were among the bearers, and that I had never seen the curate looking so cheerful.

Chapter Thirteen

Description of the injuries sustained by my father. A supremely difficult medical problem. Legal assistance of Mr Balfour Whey. Infamous decisions and public comments. A quiet church and obliging clergy. Surprising character-growth of Ezekiel. A distasteful proposition generously put forward. Disgusting behaviour of a show-room manager.

Such, then, was the incident that not only, as I have said, finally destroyed my father's health, but was also destined, after several weeks of the profoundest physical inconvenience, and almost as many months of the acutest legal anxiety, to deprive him (and ultimately myself) of the greater portion of his savings. For it was obvious from the outset that the matter had to be challenged – and indeed we had so pledged ourselves before the ambulance bore him from the vestry – at whatever cost to ourselves and our friends, and before as many tribunals as might prove necessary; and it has often seemed to me that it was only this sacred obligation that preserved my father from immediate extinction. For not only was it discovered by the three doctors, who were immediately summoned to attend upon him, that his right knee was displaying evidences of incipient synovitis, but the three falls, to which he had been subjected between the lectern and the vestry, had resulted in extremely severe contusions of both his larger gluteal muscles.

The problem before the physicians was thus an exceptionally difficult one. For while the condition of his knee demanded that he should lie upon his back, that of his gluteal muscles was even more imperative in demanding a position precisely opposed to this. After a considerable argument, therefore, it was finally decided that for the first week or ten days the position to be assumed should be a face-downwards one, with a protective cage over the contused muscles. By this means any painful pressure that might have been exerted by the bed-clothes was avoided – an additional protection being afforded by two discs of lint, previously spread with a cooling ointment. For the purposes of nourishment, which was to be ample and sustaining, my father was then to be drawn towards the end of the bed, his head being allowed to project to a sufficient distance to permit of nutriment being inserted from below. Owing to his weight, this, of course, necessitated the erection of a pulley with straps passing under his arm-pits, a return pulley with straps passing round his ankles coming into play at the end of each meal. Even with such assistance, however, my poor father's plight remained an exceedingly deplorable one; and it is scarcely to be wondered at that, from time to time, he betrayed a marked irritability.

Prostrate as he was, however, and already conscious that his career as a sidesman was definitely over, he flung himself almost immediately, and with all the energy left to him, into the necessary preliminaries of the approaching litigation. Day after day, even while still lying on his abdomen, he held prolonged interviews with Mr Balfour Whey, who most considerately lay beneath my father's bed, parallel with the sufferer and looking up into his face. Whether, in the world's history, an action of such importance – for it was fully reported in most of the daily newspapers – was ever arranged in similar circumstances I do not know, although I doubt it. But I have certainly never seen a spectacle more solemn and pathetic than that of these two earnest and horizontal men vertically discussing, across the end of the bedstead, the possible methods of legal procedure.

Nor was either to blame for the iniquitous judgements, into the details of which I do not propose to enter, but which had the effect, as I have already stated, of seriously impoverishing my poor father. For from the outset Mr Balfour Whey, although sharing to the full in my father's indignation, was explicit as to the difficulty that would certainly accrue in translating this into a legal victory. Indeed the only vehicle under which proceedings could possibly be instituted was the original and extremely crude Employers' Liability Act,* and this upon the doubtful assumption of the applicability of Sub-section (1) of Section 1, and subject to the further acceptance of the Carkeek lectern as a portion of the plant of St James-the-Least-of-All. Under this earlier Act, too, the status of the vicar as employer and that of his sidesmen as employés was far less substantiable in law than it would have been under the Workmen's Compensation Act; and deeply as I have always regretted, on general grounds, the inclusion of this latter measure in our legal machinery, I have

* 43 and 44 Vic. cap 42 (1880).

equally deplored that it was not then available to assist my poor father in his heroic crusade.

From the beginning, therefore, it was an unequal contest, with the dice of evasion loaded against my father, and all the forces of idolatry, spite, and ambition arrayed to defeat the course of justice. Thus, despite the arguments – and I have never listened to longer or more powerful ones – of the celebrated counsel that my father employed; despite the photographs – and I have never seen any more heart-rending – of the contused areas of my father's person; and despite the irrepressible applause from Simeon and myself that greeted his every reply in the witness-box, the case was not only decided against him with costs, on a series of the most palpable legal quibbles, but an appeal to a higher court met with a similarly scandalous and financially devastating result. Obviously primed, too, by the Carkeeks – although our detectives were unable to prove this – the verdict in each case became the subject of a malicious article in the *Camberwell Observer*, my father once more having to bear the total costs of the prosecutions that immediately ensued.

Nor did a printed appeal to the congregation of St James-the-Least-of-All bring my poor father more than eight shillings, although the cost of its printing and subsequent postage had amounted to no less than three pounds. Moreover – and even now the pen shakes in my hand as I force it to write the shameful words – not only was the lectern retained in the church (where it may probably be seen at this moment), but within less than a year Cosmo and Corkran Carkeek were the sons of the vicar's churchwarden. It was perhaps the bitterest stab of the whole squalid conspiracy. But my father was then too enfeebled for active resistance.

'Let it be enough,' he wrote to Alexander Carkeek, 'until at a Greater Bar you shall stand condemned, that you know, and I know, and so does your vicar, that you have committed simony in your heart.'

So ended an episode with which I have dealt thus fully – at what a cost can well be imagined – partly because, as I have said, the contemporary newspaper accounts of it were either misleading or deliberately spiteful, but chiefly because it was the means adopted by Providence of uniting us still more closely with the Stools. That this was an end possible of achievement otherwise, I have never disguised my private opinion. But since it was to lead to my own ultimate matrimony, I have always considered it best to suspend judgement; and I cannot but feel convinced that my readers will share the relief with which I now begin to approach this distant event.

For it was still distant. Let there be no mistake about that. And in the particular form in which it was about to be adumbrated, I ought not to conceal, perhaps, that for several years I found it extremely distasteful. Nevertheless, it came about, and even when Ezekiel first suggested it, deeply repugnant though the idea seemed to me, I could not help recognizing and suitably acknowledging the generosity with which it had been put forward.

'Dear Augustus,' he said, 'each of my sisters will receive an equal portion of my father's estate, and if it would be any help to you, I should be only too glad to give you one of them in marriage.'

This was on the Sunday evening, I remember, the sixth after we had lost our action against the *Camberwell Observer*, and the seventeenth after my father had been mulcted in costs by the infamous judgement of the Court of Appeal – upon which we had decided, after careful investigation, to transfer our worship to St Nicholas, Newington Butts. A quiet edifice, devoid of a lectern, yet within a few yards of the tram-lines, it had seemed to us both, although it had various drawbacks, as suitable a receptacle as we should be likely to find for the very modified degree of worship of which my father now remained capable.

'After what has happened,' he said, 'it is, of course, a subject in which I can scarcely be expected to take much further interest. But the church appears clean and its clergy seem obliging, if not particularly intelligent.'

Making it quite clear, therefore, that he would be entirely unable to accept any position of responsibility, and that his attendances, even as an ordinary worshipper, would almost certainly be precarious, my father had added his name to its list of clients, to which I had been very happy to subscribe my own. This we had done verbally, at the close of the morning service, to the obvious satisfaction of the vicar and his curate, Ezekiel having been absent, as his sisters had informed me, owing to a mild attack of gastro-enteritis. At the evening service, however, he was present as usual, and it was upon our way home together after its close that I told him of the decision to which my father and I had come, and of which we had already apprised the clergy. Transported with delight, he shook me by the hand, the hairs upon his face sparkling with happy tears, and I shall never forget the emotion with which he expressed his hope that this would complete the intimacy between us.

'Drawn together,' he said, 'in the A.D.S.U. and by your memorable salvation of me on the fifth of November, and further united in the misfortunes that have befallen the fathers of us both, surely this must be the link that shall finally unite us in a firm and irrevocable friendship.'

Deeply moved, I was unable to reply for a moment. But presently, in a response of some duration, I contrived to signify my general agreement with the aspirations that he had enunciated. He then invited me to share a second evening meal with himself, his mother and his five sisters, and it was during the progress of this that I first became aware of a new development of his character. Hitherto, as I have said, of an extremely gentle and even yielding disposition, he had now assumed, with a dignity and completeness that both surprised and delighted me, not only the headship of the table, but the full direction of the household. Thus when Faith ventured upon a remark that, on a week-day, might have been considered humorous, he at once reminded her that it was the Sabbath and gently but firmly demanded an apology; while a look from his eye was sufficient to quell Hope, who inadvertently 'hiccuped' during the pronouncement of grace. I was glad to observe, too, that these facially unattractive girls all remained seated until he had indicated that they might rise, and that together with their mother they instantly left the room when he inclined his head toward the door.

So effective, indeed, was his assumption of his

father's duties that I could not refrain from congratulating him, and it was during the conversation that naturally followed that he supplied me with details of the family finances. Thus I learned from him that, prior to his admission to the Home of Rest in which he was now detained, his father had been persuaded by his legal advisers to retire from the management of the Adult Gripe Water; and that the right to manufacture this, together with the existing plant, had been sold to a limited company. As the sole proprietor, Mr Abraham Stool had received a considerable sum of money, half of this having been paid to him in cash and the remainder in shares of the new company. The cash had then been invested, upon his solicitor's advice, in colonial and Government securities, and a will drawn up of which Ezekiel was kind enough to give me the exact particulars. Then he paused for a moment, and it was then, leaning towards me with the utmost affection, that he uttered the words of which, as I have already recorded, I could not but recognize the good feeling.

'And so you see, dear Augustus, each of my sisters will receive an equal portion of my father's estate, and if it would be any help to you, I should be only too glad to give you one of them in marriage.'

Admirably meant, however, as was this offer, and obviously one of considerable value, few could have blamed me, I think, for the instinctive shudder with which I was obliged at first to postpone an answer. Nor was he one of them.

'In fact, I never supposed,' he said, 'that you could immediately bring yourself to accept. And I fully appreciate that, had I been in your position, my gesture of repulsion would have been equally violent. But at the same time I thought it might be useful to you to know that they would be there to fall back upon.'

I stared at him.

'To fall back upon?' I asked.

Colouring deeply, he held out his hand.

'I was speaking metaphorically,' he said. 'I beg your pardon.'

'Conceded,' I replied. 'But it was an unpleasant idea.'

'And an ill-chosen phrase,' he said. 'All that I meant was that they would be there for you to select from.'

'Do you mean all of them?' I asked.

He signified his assent.

'Subject to the Great Reaper,' he said, 'I think that I can promise that.'

Then for five minutes we sat in silence, and then, extending my hand to him, I rose to my feet.

'Ezekiel,' I said, 'I am not unobliged to you, and although I could never view such a marriage with enthusiasm, yet I can conceive circumstances in which, as a last resort, it might be my duty to consider it.'

'Precisely,' he said, 'and it is for such a contingency that I shall be only too glad, as I have said, to reserve them.'

Then we parted, Ezekiel, as he afterwards told me, to the happy contemplation of our closer friendship, and myself, as I walked home, to the sombre consideration of the possibilities with which I had been presented. I had scarcely been so occupied, however, for ten minutes when I suddenly became aware of the odour of alcohol, and to my infinite horror found myself being embraced by the show-room manager from Paternoster Row.

'Why, ShAugustus,' he said. 'Fansheen you.'

Involuntarily I recoiled from him, but he came after me.

'Fansheen you,' he repeated. 'Hahu?'

And having kissed me, he sat down on the pavement.

Chapter Fourteen

Person and character of Mr Archibald Maidstone. Irreverent attitude towards the firm's publications. Would-be laxity of two constables. Their tardy performance of an obvious duty. Deplorable condition of my Sunday trousers. Their effect on Miss Botterill and Mr Chrysostom Lorton. The arrival and influence of the Reverend Eugene Cake. Mr Maidstone is dismissed and I succeed him. Complete discomfiture of his three elder children.

I have said that he sat down, and even had that been all, it would have been a sufficiently unpleasant encounter, although, as I had instantly seen, it ought certainly to issue in my own immediate commercial advancement. But he did more, for so firmly did he grip my arm that I was compelled to sit down beside him, with what reluctance will be the better imagined when I have briefly described his person and character. By name Archibald Maidstone, he was a tall, gaunt man with high cheek-bones and a grey moustache, and in his earlier life he had held some sort of position in the British mercantile marine. An accident at sea, however, had deprived him of one of his eyes as well as of the two middle fingers of his left hand, and for some time he had been the proprietor of a small and unsuccessful marine store. He had then become a commercial traveller for a firm of grocers that had subsequently failed, and had finally, at the age of forty-one, obtained a minor position in the business of Mr Chrysostom Lorton.

A married man with several children, he had afterwards been appointed show-room manager, and it was as his assistant, as I have already said, that I had entered Mr Lorton's employment. From the outset, however, although I had endeavoured to conceal this, I had both disliked and distrusted him, and in spite of what I presumed to be a species of nautical humour, I had found his attitude towards me peculiarly offensive. I had never been accustomed, for example, as I had been obliged to point out to him, to be addressed as 'young-feller-me-lad', or 'the bosun's mate', and I had even been compelled to report him to Mr Lorton in order to secure more respectful treatment. I had been deeply concerned, too, to observe the levity with which, in the absence of customers, he would handle and describe the sacred publications of which it was his privilege to be the salesman. 'Bilge-water for the Bairns', for instance, was a frequent expression of his for our well-known series of *Talks with the Infants*, and I had even heard him refer to a parcel of *Claudie's Temptations* as 'another half-hundredweight of the Prigs' Paradise'. Indeed, on one occasion, ignorant of the presence of the author – the celebrated Non-conformist, the Reverend Eugene Cake – he had tossed me a window-copy of *Without are Dogs*, saying that, if they were 'wise bow-wows', they would stay there; and it was only after a second interview with Mr Chrysostom Lorton, the tearful intervention of Mrs Maidstone, and a complete apology to the Reverend Cake, that he was allowed to retain his position.

But for the fact, indeed, that his children were still at school and dependent upon his earnings, and that his wife, who seemed inexplicably attached to him, had been an invalid for some years, he would most certainly have been dismissed, and I had always felt that this should have been done. Nor was I alone in this, for when I ventured to congratulate him on the successful sale of *Without are Dogs*, the Reverend Cake had entirely agreed with me in deploring Mr Maidstone's retention in the business.

Such, then, was the man by whose side I was now sitting upon the damp pavement, and from whom I only detached myself after a prolonged struggle, just as a member of the police force came in sight. This was a stalwart constable of somewhat coarse appearance to whom I immediately made myself known, and to whose attention I then brought Mr Maidstone, who was still seated upon the pavement.

'Ha, I see,' he said, 'a bit sideways. Do you happen to know where the gentleman lives?'

'I don't know the street,' I said, 'nor can I accept your assumption that such a degenerate can be called a gentleman. But I understand that his home is in Greenwich.'

'Num shixteen,' said Mr Maidstone.

The constable bent over him, and raised him to his feet.

'Now, come along,' he said. 'Pull yourself together.'

Mr Maidstone swayed for a moment and then saluted us.

'Happit meetu,' he said. 'Num shixteen.'

'Sixteen what?' said the constable.

'Manshtroad,' said Mr Maidstone. 'Shixteen Manshtroad, Grinsh.'

Then he toppled forward into the constable's arms, but recovered himself and smiled at us affectionately.

The constable turned to me.

'Well, if I was you, sir, I'd put him in a cab and take him home.'

I stared at him in utter amazement.

'But do you mean to say,' I inquired, 'that you aren't going to take him in charge?'

'Oh, no need, sir,' he said, 'seeing as you know the gentleman – not if you'll put him into a cab and take him home.'

'But, my good man,' I said, 'how can I do that? It's a quarter past ten, and I'm going home to bed.'

'Well, we can't leave him here,' said the constable, 'or he'll be getting into trouble. What about givin' 'im a 'and to your own 'ouse, sir?'

'To my own house?' I cried. 'A person in that condition?'

The constable pushed his helmet back and scratched his forehead.

'Well, it'd be doin' 'im a good turn, sir,' he said, 'seein' as 'ow the gentleman's a friend of yours.'

'On the contrary,' I said, 'he's neither a friend of mine, nor do I propose to condone his infamy.'

Here Mr Maidstone caught hold of the constable.

'Shinfamous thing,' he said. 'Carncondonit.'

Then he sat down again and began to sing a hymn, just as a second constable came round the corner; and after conferring for a moment, they approached me once more with the suggestion that they should conduct Mr Maidstone to Angela Gardens.

'You see, sir,' they said, 'we don't want to make no

trouble, and maybe some day you'll want a 'and yourself.'

For a moment, so casually were the words spoken, I scarcely realized their astounding import. But when I did so, it was, of course, instantly clear to me that I must define my position once and for all. Drawing myself up, therefore, I addressed the two constables with all the firmness of which I was capable.

'You have chosen to be insolent,' I said, 'and for that you may rest assured I shall report you to your superiors at my earliest convenience. But I must have you understand, now and for ever, and beyond all possibility of future cavil, that I entirely and absolutely refuse to associate myself with any evasion of the law of this land. This person, whose name is Archibald Maidstone, who is employed by Mr Chrysostom Lorton of Paternoster Row, and whose home, if I have interpreted him rightly, is in Manchester Road, Greenwich, is not only drunk, but, as his actions have proclaimed him, is also disorderly in every sense. As a Xtian gentleman, therefore, no less than as a citizen, whose trousers have been soiled by his agency, I demand that you shall do your duty by removing him to the appropriate place of detention. And I would further have you note that I am aware of both your numbers and shall certainly inform myself of your procedure.'

'Hear, hear,' said Mr Maidstone, 'more. Thashway talk to 'em. Manshtroad, Grinsh.'

Then the constables conferred again, and stooping over Mr Maidstone, lifted him once more from the pavement.

'Very good, sir,' they said, 'if you can't see your way

to look after him, we shall have to take him to the station.'

I bowed to them coldly.

'Since that was so plainly your duty,' I said, 'I can only regret your tardy perception of it.'

It will thus be seen that, harassed as I was by the problem provided for me by Ezekiel Stool, I was now confronted with the much more immediate one of purging Mr Lorton's business of Mr Archibald Maidstone. For to me, at any rate, it was imperatively clear that such a person could not possibly remain in it without imperilling the whole of the spiritual prestige that was perhaps its most lucrative asset. At the same time, however, as I also saw, the preliminaries to expulsion would require very careful handling, owing to the choleric temper, the extreme vanity, and the peculiar limitations of Mr Chrysostom himself.

After what can well be imagined, therefore, was a restless night, and not without the profoundest consideration, I decided upon the seat of my Sunday trousers as the best introduction to the subject in hand; and it was with this in view that I refrained from dusting or drying them and carried them to the city with me the next morning.

Nor was I disappointed. For not only did Miss Botterill, my female inferior, visibly recoil from them, but they instantly caught the eye of Mr Chrysostom Lorton as he crossed the show-room on the way to his office. Indeed, disposed as they were, with the seat uppermost, upon one corner of the right-hand counter, it would have been difficult for even the most preoccupied to have passed them without notice, and especially as the moisture that had been transferred to them from the pavement was now being illuminated by the morning sun. Nor was the effect of them upon Mr Chrysostom Lorton less than it had been upon Miss Botterill. Starting back, almost as if he had been lassoed, he stood for a moment staring at them with dilated pupils, and then very softly he approached them on tiptoe with the point of his umbrella extended before him.

'Good God,' he said, 'whose are those?'

With an appropriate gesture I signified their ownership. He turned to Miss Botterill.

'Fetch me a chair,' he said.

She pushed one towards him with averted eyes. He fell back into it and waved his hand.

'Take them away,' he said. 'Put them somewhere else.'

I removed them from the counter and placed them underneath it.

'Where's Mr Maidstone?' he said.

I replied that he had not come.

'I imagine,' I said, 'that he has been detained.'

'Detained?' he cried. 'Why should he be detained? What should have detained him? It's ten past nine.'

'Even so,' I replied.

'Then kindly inform me,' he went on, 'why you have taken advantage of his absence.'

I looked at him gravely.

'I am not aware,' I said, 'of having done any such thing.'

'Not aware?' he said. 'Not aware, sir? Where's Miss Botterill? Put this chair back.'

He rose to his feet and stood glaring at me, still

pointing his umbrella at the counter.

'Then do you mean to tell me,' he said, 'that if Mr Maidstone had been present, your disgusting wearing apparel would still have been there?'

I bowed my head.

'I cannot say,' I replied. 'But it was to call his attention to them that I had placed them on the counter.'

He lowered his umbrella.

'To call his attention to them? But what has Mr Maidstone to do with your trousers?'

'In this particular case,' I said, 'a very great deal, since he was solely responsible for their condition.'

He opened his mouth.

'Mr Maidstone?' he gasped.

'Mr Archibald Maidstone,' I said, 'your show-room manager.'

'But good God,' he said, 'you don't mean to tell me that he's in the habit of borrowing your trousers?'

'Unfortunately,' I replied, 'that was not necessary. I was myself occupying them on the occasion in question.'

'But I don't understand,' he said. 'Where's Miss Botterill? Bring me that chair back. I want to sit down.'

She brought back the chair, and just as she did so, the street door opened to admit a newcomer – none other, indeed, than the Reverend Eugene Cake, bearing the typescript of his new novel.*

It was an important entrance. But Mr Chrysostom still sat staring at the counter, and having greeted Mr Cake rather perfunctorily, demanded a further

* *Gnashers of Teeth.*

inspection of the trousers. Once again, therefore, I placed them upon the counter, and once again Miss Botterill recoiled, the Reverend Eugene Cake recoiling also and dropping the typescript of his novel.

'Now,' said Mr Chrysostom, 'you have already informed me that you were encased in these nauseating garments, and you have further asserted that Mr Maidstone was solely responsible for their present condition. Mr Maidstone, you tell me, is probably detained somewhere, and it is now a quarter past nine. I may be unintelligent. I may be obtuse. I may be unfit to conduct this business. But I don't understand it, sir. I don't understand it. Where's Miss Botterill? Get Mr Cake a chair.'

With her hand over her face, Miss Botterill ran across the show-room and returned with a chair for Mr Cake. Mr Chrysostom glanced at him.

'Are you comfortable, Cake?'

The Reverend Eugene bowed a little stiffly.

'Very well, then,' said Mr Chrysostom. 'Very well, I repeat. And now you must explain, sir. You must explain. I don't want to pre-judge you. I never pre-judge anybody. But I don't like it, sir. I don't like it. And you must allow me to remind you that this is not the first time that you have obliged me to discuss your trousers.'

'Sir,' I replied, 'I am deeply aware of it, and none can regret it more than myself, nor the painful circumstances that you have, I think justly, now compelled me to disclose.'

I then very briefly, but with all essential details, described my encounter with Mr Maidstone, concluding with the numbers of the two constables and a surmise that he was being detained to see the magistrate.

When I had finished, Mr Chrysostom was breathing heavily, while Mr Cake was engaged in silent prayer. Then they both rose and stood with their backs to the trousers while Mr Chrysostom gave his orders.

'Miss Botterill,' he said, 'when Mr Maidstone arrives, you will please request him to come to my room. Mr Carp, having removed your trousers, you will kindly take charge of the show-room.'

Colouring deeply, Mr Cake touched him on the arm. 'I suppose you refer,' he said, 'to the trousers on the counter.'

'Eh, what?' said Mr Chrysostom. 'Yes, yes, of course. The trousers on the counter. You didn't suppose –?'

'I endeavoured not to,' said Mr Cake. 'But perhaps it would have been better to be more explicit.'

Slightly ruffled, however, as was the eminent novelist by the occasion and manner of his reception, he was completely emphatic, as he afterwards assured me, on the necessity for dismissing Mr Maidstone; and indeed Mr Chrysostom, as he also informed me, had needed very little in the way of persuasion.

'In fact, I think I may say,' he said, a couple of hours later, as he passed through the show-room on his way to the street, 'that *Gnashers of Teeth* will find a good friend in Mr Maidstone's successor.'

I clasped his hand.

'I sincerely hope so,' I said.

'It's even more powerful,' he said, 'than *Without are Dogs*.'

It was in this fashion, then, that I became show-room manager with an added, though insufficient emolument, for Mr Maidstone, when he arrived the next morning, was at once dismissed after a brief interview. Explaining at first that he had failed to attend owing to a very violent bilious headache, he was, of course, unable, when pressed by Mr Chrysostom, to deny the truth of my allegations; and it subsequently emerged that, after a night in the police station, he had been fined ten shillings by the local magistrate. Nor did his resentment, when he came downstairs again, assume the physical character that I had feared, although I had taken the precaution of keeping Miss Botterill beside me and holding my police whistle in my left hand. On the contrary, he seemed to recognize not only the grossness of his delinquency, but the inevitable nature of the consequences that had so rightly ensued.

'Well, you've done me in, laddie,' he said. 'But I suppose I deserved it.'

'I regret to say,' I replied, 'that there can be no doubt of it.'

'But it's going to be hard,' he added, 'on the wife and family.'

'The wages of sin,' I said, 'are never easy.'

Then Miss Botterill sniffed and pulled out her hand-kerchief, and Mr Maidstone closed the street door, and but for a diverting sequel upon the following Friday, the incident closed very satisfactorily. Upon that morning, however, Mr Maidstone's three elder children, a girl and two boys, all apparently under fourteen, entered the show-room and peremptorily demanded to be taken upstairs to Mr Chrysostom Lorton. By names, Polly,

Arthur, and George, they had come to apply for their father's reinstatement, chiefly, as they alleged, on account of their mother, whom they described as suffering from pulmonary consumption. Needless to say, much to their obvious discomfiture, Mr Chrysostom refused to see them, and after a brief consultation, they filed out again very much more humbly than they had come in. Unpleasant children, it was an amusing episode, and I could not help laughing somewhat heartily, although Polly, who appeared to be the eldest, made a grimace at me as she went out.

Chapter Fifteen

Happy years. A typical day. Simeon Whey is at last ordained. His first sermon at St Sepulchre's, Balham. Intensive campaign of the A.D.S.U. I meet Miss Moonbeam and call her Mary. Affecting appeal not to leave her in darkness. I promise not to do so. A face to lean on. Will I come again? Adventure on the stage of the Empresses Theatre.

I have said that this incident ended satisfactorily, but, as I shall very shortly have to demonstrate, it was subsequently to become associated with what I have always regarded as the most tragic event of my career – an event so annihilating in its ultimate consequences, and so misunderstood in its immediate details, that few less proven and resilient characters could have emerged from it unimpaired. Nor could my physique, I think, have stood the strain but for the four or five years that now intervened, during which I was enabled, in a life of comparative calm, to add very considerably to my bodily weight. Indeed in many respects, uneventful as they were, these were amongst the happiest years of my earlier manhood, and I cannot do better, perhaps, than describe for the benefit of my readers a typical day of this period of my life.

Required, like my father, who was still fortunately able to pursue his secular avocations, to be present at my place of employment by nine o'clock in the morning, my mother would call me at a quarter past seven, bringing a cup of tea to my bedside. This I would permit to cool for three or four minutes while I ate one of the biscuits with which it was accompanied; and then, sitting up in bed with my dressing-gown over my shoulders, I would drink the upper half of it before again eating. I would then eat the second of my two biscuits, and having drunk the remainder of the tea, would ring for my mother, who would then bring my hot water prior to the removal of the tea-things.

I was now ready to dress, and pushing down the bed-clothes, would begin by leaning forward and reaching the trousers which, the night before, I had hung over the end of the bed, with this very purpose in view. Containing my pants, to the lower extremities of which my socks would be still adherent, I was thus enabled, without removing my nightgown, to clothe my lower limbs before actually rising; and it was only then that I would finally leave the bed and cross the room towards the wash-hand stand. I would then fill the basin, leaving sufficient hot water for the purposes of subsequent shaving, and having locked the door and drawn the blinds would remove my nightgown preparatory to washing.

It would now be half-past seven, and if it were at all cold, I would don my vest before bending over the basin, never failing, however, in even the severest weather, to roll up my sleeves as far as my elbows. Then having dried and put on my shirt, I would shave before putting on my shirt-front, always brushing my hair before I put on my coat, but not before putting on my waistcoat. I would then select a clean handkerchief from my top right-hand drawer, and having pulled up my trousers a little to prevent them from becoming baggy, would kneel by my bedside at seven forty-five, assuming an erect position again at five minutes to eight. I would then pull up the blinds, open the windows, fold up my nightgown and put it in my nightgown bag, and by eight o'clock would be sitting at the harmonium in readiness to burst into the morning hymn.

Thus begun, and breakfast having been concluded, the day would next behold me inside an omnibus, unless the weather were warm enough to permit of my sitting upon the top for the purpose of rebuking adjacent smokers; and punctually at nine o'clock, I would enter the show-room and divest myself of my hat, scarf and overcoat. I would then exchange a courteous word or two with Miss Botterill and the youth who had succeeded me as show-room assistant, and immediately apply myself to the various duties that as show-room manager devolved upon my shoulders. Comprising the arrangement of books upon the shelves and counters, as well as of an attractive display in the street window, these would include, of course, my personal attendance upon the more important of our retail customers, the booking of orders, the checking of the show-room takings, and the maintenance of discipline amongst my two subordinates. And I had long ago proved the necessity, in view of such diverse demands, of paying the utmost attention to my physical upkeep.

At eleven o'clock, therefore, I would despatch Miss Botterill to a neighbouring branch of the Aerated Bread Company for a glass of hot milk and a substantial slice of a cake appropriately known as lunch cake. I would then, at twelve thirty, repair in person to the same branch of this valuable company, where I would generally order from one of the quieter waitresses a double portion of sausages and mashed potatoes, accompanied by a cup of coffee, and followed by an apple dumpling or a segment of baked jam roll. This was the more necessary because the hour from one to two was usually the busiest of the working day, while from two to three, when my subordinates lunched in turn, I had, of course, only one of them to assist me.

By three o'clock, however, they had both returned, and I would take the opportunity, five minutes later, of again sending Miss Botterill to the Aerated Bread Company for my mid-afternoon cup of tea. This I would drink, unthickened by food, but at half-past four I would send her out for another cup, and with this I would eat a roll and butter, a small dish of honey, and perhaps a single doughnut. Thus fortified I would then continue at work until six o'clock, when the show-room closed, and at half-past six I was sitting down at home to the chief meal of the evening. Taken somewhat earlier than had been my father's custom in the days of my boyhood and adolescence, I had found myself obliged to insist on the alteration in view of the many demands upon my evening hours. Most of my active work, for example, at the doors of public-houses, required an attendance from seven to nine, while few of the local prayer-meetings began at a later hour than half-past seven or eight.

Early as was this meal, however, it was none the less welcome, consisting as it usually did of a joint and two vegetables followed by a wholesome pudding, tea, bread and jam, and perhaps a slice or two of home-made cake. Then after evening prayers, I would embrace my father, who was now always in bed by a quarter to nine, and leave the house upon some such holy errand as I have described in the previous paragraph. I did not fail, however, on returning home to drink a bowl of arrowroot and eat some digestive biscuits, and whenever possible, in the interests of my health, I would retire to my bedroom at ten fifteen.

Here I would find my windows closed for the night, the blinds drawn for the sake of decency, a jug of hot water standing in my basin, while a hot-water bottle would be within the bed. All would be in readiness, therefore, for my quick disrobing, a process that I would begin as soon as I had locked the door; and within five minutes, I would be bending over the basin clad as I have described myself some fifteen hours earlier. I would then brush my teeth, using some mild disinfectant, open my nightgown bag and extract my nightgown, and having taken off my vest, would slip on my nightgown prior to the removal of my lower garments. These I would then detach from myself with a single downward movement, subsequently hanging them over the end of the bed, after which I would put on my dressing-gown and bedroom slippers and utter a brief but fervent supplication. I would then pull up the blinds so that the stars could shine upon my bed, swallow a tablespoon of the Adult Gripe Water, unlock the door, extinguish the light, and by ten thirty-five be composed for slumber.

Such was a typical day of this period of my life,

during which, as I have said, I increased in weight, and in which, as I am glad to believe, my moral stature also expanded and became consolidated. This was, at any rate, the conviction of my friend Simeon Whey, who took the opportunity of my twenty-sixth birthday to describe me in his diary as 'now in the full flower of his southern Metropolitan Xtian manhood'. Indeed, the whole passage is well worth transcribing, written as it was on the eve of his ordination, and following a happy hour together discussing the price-lists of various clerical tailors.

'By a moving coincidence,' he wrote, 'the eve of my ordination has coincided with the twenty-sixth birthday of my old and dear friend Augustus Carp of Angela Gardens. And yet perhaps old is scarcely the right word, for mature as he is, he is now in the full flower of his southern Metropolitan Xtian manhood. Nor have I ever seen him looking so large as when he came to see me at 2.35 to receive the hand-painted toothbrush, with which I had promised to present him, and to give me his benediction for the morrow. Fully a stone heavier than this time last year, his moustache has become noticeably more abundant, and his every movement possesses the weight and gravity of a man twenty years his senior. Admirable as was his diction, too, even as a boy, it has now attained a level of sonorous grandeur, from which it never lapses in even the most trivial pronouncements imposed upon him by necessary human intercourse. Is it surprising, therefore, that I daily thank P,* for so noble and inspiring an example?'

* Providence

Dear Simeon, loyal and appreciative, for many a long
year hadst thou been trying to get ordained, but now
thou hadst succeeded, and well do I remember thy first
sermon at St Sepulchre's, Balham. Cast thy bread, thou
preachedst, upon the waters, for thou shalt find it after
many days – and mark, thou didst say, it is not
demanded of us to cast our jewels or financial securities.
No, no, thou saidst, it was well recognized that the
former would sink and the latter become unintelligible,
whereas bread was nutriment for the fishes of the deep,
and in due course would return to our tables. Moreover,
bread was cheap, thou didst say, and even the poorest of
us was sometimes tempted to waste his bread, and for
him there was a message – kck – in these beautiful
words to place his bread, as it were, out at interest. Let
us all, then, take heed, thou saidst, never to waste our
bread but to collect it earnestly with both hands, and
whenever we saw any water, yea, no matter how little, to
cast it upon it in faith fearing not. And then it would
return to us, if not in the form of fish, then in some
other form which we wotted not of. For what was bred
in the bone could never be cast down, nay, not until
seventy times seven.

Good Simeon, such was thy first sermon, and I
doubt if thou hast ever preached a better.

Little as we dreamed it, however, Providence was
now hurrying towards me with the heaviest cross of my
adult life, a cross so heavy that even now I cannot help
shuddering at its weight, and one that compelled me
not only to retire from business, but to remove from
Camberwell to Stoke Newington. Nor was it less bitter
in that the instrument of deposit was a young and

exceptionally attractive female, with whom I had been brought into contact in the course of my work for the Anti-Dramatic and Saltatory Union.

This was about a year after Simeon's ordination and soon after I had inaugurated, in my capacity as Vice-President, an intensive campaign of personal exhortation at all the most notorious West End theatres. Thus I had arranged that there should be posted at the stage entrances of all these more popular haunts of vice earnest young workers of the male sex plentifully provided with the Union's literature. These would then approach the in-coming actors and actresses with a few well-chosen words of warning, pointing out to them the iniquity of their occupation and inviting them to embrace some other profession. Having had our evening meals, Ezekiel and myself would each then visit a group of theatres to encourage our representatives and lend them the personal aid of our riper experience and more gifted oratory.

This, then, was the occasion of my being present at about half-past seven on a January evening at the stage door of the Empresses Theatre, where a play called *The Peach Girl* was about to be performed. This was a drama, accompanied by music, and frequently interrupted, I believe, by amatory dances, which had already been presented nearly three hundred times and was still attracting enormous audiences. I had not myself seen it, but Ezekiel, who had witnessed a considerable portion of it before making his protest at its first performance, had particularly deplored the abbreviated costumes of most of the female dancers. He had made an exception, however, in favour of the

Ezekiel Stool, drawn from a portrait once
in the possession of the A.D.S.U.

principal actress, by whose singular beauty he had been greatly impressed, and in whom he had discerned, he thought, in spite of her surroundings, an appreciable degree of natural goodness. By name Mary Moonbeam, she had been assigned the part, it appeared, of a quite simple seller of fruit, to whom a naval officer, accompanied upon the stage by a large number of female midshipmen, had immediately begun, in a voluptuous baritone, to address words of affection.

What had happened subsequently Ezekiel did not, of course, know, since he had then made his protest and been compelled to leave. But he had felt assured, from the sweetness of her expression, that she had been more sinned against than sinning, and that in other surroundings she might easily have developed into an almost ideal district visitor. On the other hand, it was quite clear, from the letter-press outside the theatre, that she was the chief attraction of the play, and she had twice refused to discuss her future with our young representative at the stage door.

It was with as open a mind, therefore, as it was at all possible for me to possess in respect of an actress, that I perceived her alighting from an expensive-looking vehicle soon after I had reached the stage door. Nor was I at first able, owing to the speed of her movements – she was ten minutes later, it appeared, than usual – and the voluminous furs, in which she had ensconced herself, to obtain a clear view of her face. In fact, when I first touched her, she brushed me aside, and it was only after she had glanced at me a second time that she stopped for a moment and began to stare at me with her exceptionally limpid, hazel eyes.

'Hullo,' she said, 'you're not the same man.'

'I am the Vice-President,' I said, 'of the Anti-Dramatic Union.'

'And Saltatory,' she said. 'Don't forget the Saltatory part.'

'Would that it were possible,' I replied. 'But it isn't.'

She gave a little sigh.

'No, I suppose not,' she said, 'not with all us girls earning our living by it.'

'And hurling others,' I said, 'to their deaths.'

'Oh, no,' she said, 'not really?'

'Every night,' I replied, 'in thousands and thousands.'

'Oh, good gracious,' she said, 'not every night?'

I nodded gravely.

'Every night,' I said, 'in thousands and thousands and thousands and thousands.'

'But goodness me,' she cried, 'that's more than ever.'

'It's more and more,' I said, 'every night.'

'Well, I never,' she said. 'What a fearful mortality.'

'Fearful indeed,' I replied, 'and you are responsible.'

'Oh, my aunt,' she said, 'how perfectly horrible. Can't you come and talk to me after the first act?'

'I should be only too glad,' I said, 'if you would tell me where to come.'

'Oh, anybody'll tell you,' she said. 'Nine fifteen.'

Then she disappeared, and at a quarter past nine, when I returned to the theatre after consulting Ezekiel, I was eventually shown into a small room, where she appeared to be undressing herself to a marked extent. She waved her hand, however, and bade me take a chair, assuring me that the worst was already over, and

167

introducing me to a woman, whom she described as her dresser, and whose name was Mrs Montgomery.

'This is Mr Carp,' she said, 'the Vice-President of the Anti-Dramatic and Saltatory Union.'

Mrs Montgomery wiped her hands on her apron prior to greeting me with great cordiality.

'Happy to meet you,' she said. 'I've read a lot of your tracts, and mark my words, there's a lot of truth in 'em.'

'Yes,' said Miss Moonbeam, 'and isn't it awful, Bags?* He says we kill thousands of people every night.'

'Well, I shouldn't wonder,' said Mrs Montgomery, 'not for a moment, I shouldn't. What with this modern dancing and all. Hold your chin up, dearie.'

She was applying some powder to Miss Moonbeam's neck, and presently stood back a little, eyeing her critically.

'Yes,' said Miss Moonbeam. 'But oughtn't we to do something? It doesn't seem right just to let it go on.'

'Oh, no,' I cried. 'Nor it is. Nor it is, Miss Moonbeam. Believe me.'

'I do,' she said. 'I do believe you. Get out of the light, Bags. I want to look at him.'

For a moment I sat in silence, permitting her to feast her eyes. Then she bent forward a little, holding out her hands.

'Oh, Mr Carp,' she said, 'I'm only a poor actress. Help me to be better. Help me to be like you.'

Withdrawing my gloves and putting them in my left-hand pocket, I advanced towards her and took hold of her hands.

* Presumably an abbreviation of Montgomery.

'My dear Miss Moonbeam,' I said.

But she looked at me rather pathetically.

'Oh, Mr Carp,' she said, 'won't you call me Mary?'

I considered for a moment. It was a difficult position. For though I could not help feeling that she was a little presumptuous, I had to remember that this was probably the first occasion on which she had met a really good man. I therefore decided to grant her petition.

'My dear Mary,' I said, 'I shall be only too happy.'

She breathed a sigh and removed her hands.

'Oh, how lovely of you,' she said. 'Now I must go on dressing.'

'But, my dear Mary,' I said, 'is that necessary?'

'Oh, I think so,' she said. 'You see, if I didn't –'

I waved my hand.

'I'm afraid you've misunderstood me,' I said.

'Very likely,' she said. 'I'm so stupid. But you're going to help me, Mr Carp, aren't you?'

I bowed sympathetically.

'Nothing could please me more,' I said, 'than to lead you out of darkness into the membership of our Union. But would it not be better to rise up at once – to rise up at once, I say, and come away?'

But she shook her head.

'You see, I'm bound by a contract,' she said, 'and I have to support rather a large family.'

Involuntarily I staggered a little.

'But, Mary,' I cried.

'Brothers and sisters,' she explained. 'I'm paying for their education.'

Profoundly relieved, and not a little touched, I

regained my equilibrium and invited her to confide in me. Her mother was dead, it appeared, and her father had been unfortunate and was now unable to provide for his children.

'And so they batten,' I said, 'on your ill-gotten earnings.'

She turned and looked at me for a moment in silence. Then she smiled again as she put on her slippers.

'You seem to understand things,' she said, 'so quickly.'

Then a small boy looked round the door.

'Curtain's up, miss,' he said, and disappeared again.

'Oh dear, oh dear,' she cried, 'how the time flies. Can't you come and talk to me after the show?'

I smiled at her not unkindly.

'By ten fifteen,' I said, 'I shall be in my bedroom.'

'But what am I to do?' she said. 'I've begun to lean on you. You aren't going to leave me here wallowing?'

I stared at her.

'Wallowing in what?' I asked.

'Why, in the darkness,' she said, 'killing all those people.'

I took her hands again.

'My dear Mary,' I said, 'it is in order to remove you that I am here.'

She gave a little sigh.

'Oh, I was sure I could trust you,' she said. 'I knew I could trust you, the moment I saw you.'

'Yes, it's his face,' said Mrs Montgomery. 'Isn't it, dearie? It's one of those faces one wants to lean on.

'Oh yes, yes,' she cried, 'with all one's weight. Couldn't you bring it round tomorrow after the matinée? And then very likely you'll meet some of my friends, and perhaps you'll be able to remove us all.'

'But not before six,' I said, 'or a quarter past.

'That'll do nicely,' she said. 'There's my call.'

Then she ran from the room, just as an electric bell began to sound in the corner, and Mrs Montgomery was kind enough to tell me the quickest way to leave the theatre.

Unfortunately, however, she was either inaccurate, or by some odd chance I failed to understand her, for a moment later I found myself on the stage, just as the naval officer was about to embrace Miss Moonbeam. By a curious coincidence, too, my appearance synchronized with the dramatic utterance by Miss Moonbeam of the words, 'Hush, Reginald, he comes,' which added for the moment to my perplexity. For while it was possible (and this proved to be the case) that the words bore reference to some fellow-actor, it was also possible, I thought, that she might have been informing him of my own presence in the theatre. Nor could I be certain from the attitude of the audience, as it unanimously rose with roars of applause, that my recent efforts to rescue their favourite might not have become known to it and touched its heart. I conceived it my duty, therefore, without prejudicing my position, to make a courteous bow or two before retiring, and I took the opportunity of handing the naval officer an illustrated copy of *Did Wycliffe Waltz?*

Chapter Sixteen

*Disappointing attitude of Ezekiel. Suggested nuptials of Miss
Moonbeam. An occasion for tact and postponement. I am obliged
to write a letter. Ezekiel accompanies me to the Empresses
Theatre. We are a little taken aback by the numbers to be
rescued. An apparently delightful beverage. I address Miss
Moonbeam's friends on the subject of temperance. Ezekiel
addresses them on the evils of the drama. We arrange a meeting.
Description of meeting.*

Afterwards, as I have suggested, I was to discover in Miss
Moonbeam an almost incredible capacity for evil. But
that night, as I emerged from the theatre into the anxious
arms of Ezekiel Stool, I could not help feeling in the
utmost agreement with him as to her character and
physical appearance. Indeed so complete was my
endorsement both of his judgement and prevision that I
must confess to having been a little surprised by his
reception of my news.

'So you're meeting her again?' he said.

'Yes, tomorrow evening,' I replied, 'when I hope to
draw closer to her in every way.'

He stopped abruptly and began to peer at me
suspiciously through the dense tangle that now covered
his face.

'How do you mean closer?' he said.

I waved my hand.

'She has so much to learn,' I said, 'so much to
understand. She's like a little child, Ezekiel, just as you
supposed – a female child that has never been properly
taught.'

'Yes, very likely,' he said. 'But why shouldn't I teach her myself? I'm the president of the Union after all.'

'But, my dear Ezekiel,' I said, 'undoubted as are your gifts both as organizer and financier of our movement, do you really consider that you have quite the personality for such intimate soul-work as Miss Moonbeam requires?'

'Absolutely,' said Ezekiel.

'Then I can only say,' I replied, 'that I fail to agree with you.'

It was an awkward moment, and it was not until the third attempt that Ezekiel succeeded in making himself intelligible.

'And so you mean to imply,' he said, 'that for the purposes of approaching Miss Moonbeam, your personality is superior to mine?'

I touched his arm, not without affection.

'Or shall we rather say,' I replied, 'that it is more attractive?'

'But I deny it,' he cried. 'I deny it most passionately. I deny it with every fibre of my being.'

I withdrew my glove for a moment from his coat-sleeve.

'But, my dear Ezekiel,' I said, 'that doesn't alter the position.'

'The position?' he said. 'What position?'

'Why, the position,' I replied, 'between Mary and myself.'

For a moment the silence was almost terrifying. Then he dropped his umbrella, and I put my foot upon it.

'Between who?' he said. 'Between who?'

'Between Mary,' I repeated, 'and myself.'

'But do you mean to tell me,' he cried, 'that as Vice-President – as Vice-President, I say, of a Union such as ours –'

I touched his sleeve again.

'Or shall we say *an* Union, seeing that Union begins with a vowel?'

But he stamped his foot, evidently losing self-control.

'No, we won't,' he screamed. 'We won't say *an* Union. Why should we say *an* Union if we don't want to? We don't say *an* Youth or *an* Yew-tree.'

'Simply,' I replied, 'because the two latter words happen to be inaugurated with a consonant.'

'But I deny it,' he shouted. 'I deny it most passionately. I deny it with every fibre of my being.'

For a moment I stood aghast. Hitherto I had been conciliatory. But here was a question upon which there could be no compromise.

'But, Ezekiel Stool,' I said, 'as man to man – nay, as Xtian gentleman to Xtian gentleman – do you mean to tell me that you are prepared to deny that the word Yew-tree begins with a Y?'

'No, I don't,' he said, 'I deny it completely. I deny it with all the vehemence at my command.'

But I held up my hand.

'Just a moment,' I said. 'This is a matter, Ezekiel, upon which I must be absolutely clear. Do you mean to deny that the word does begin with a Y? Or do you mean to deny that you meant to tell me that you were prepared to deny that it did?'

'I deny it all,' said Ezekiel. 'I deny the whole thing.'

'But, my dear Ezekiel,' I said, 'that is impossible.'

'But how can it be impossible,' he said, 'if I've just done it?'

'Because the two alternatives,' I replied, 'are contradictory.'

'Then I deny them both,' he said. 'I deny them utterly. I deny them to the utmost limit of my capacity.'

'But by denying one,' I said, 'you affirm the other, and by denying the other you affirm the first.'

'Then I deny neither,' he said. 'I deny neither of them. I deny neither of them to my last breath.'

'Then you affirm both?' I asked.

'Absolutely and entirely,' he said, 'to the remotest follicle of my manhood.'

'But that leaves us,' I said, 'just as we were.'

'Very likely,' he replied. 'I don't know.'

'But I don't understand,' I said.

'Nor do I,' he said.

We stood staring at one another in silence.

'Then we'd better go back,' I said, 'to the original Yew-tree.'

'What Yew-tree?' inquired Ezekiel.

'Why, the one you referred to,' I said, 'as not requiring an *an*.'

'But I've already told you,' he said, 'that I deny that.'

'But, my dear Ezekiel,' I said, 'you can't deny things like that.'

'I not only can,' he said, 'but I do.'

'But you'll soon be denying,' I cried, 'that I'm the Vice-President of the Anti-Dramatic and Saltatory Union.'

'I certainly shall,' he said, 'if you continue to go about referring to actresses by their Xtian names.'

'But, my dear Ezekiel,' I said, 'it was entirely at her own request that I referred to Miss Moonbeam as Mary.'

He stepped back a pace, obviously shaken.

'Do you mean to tell me,' he said, 'that she asked you to?'

'Most certainly,' I replied, 'and if you would like to hear them, I can repeat her actual words.'

'Please do,' he said.

'"Oh, Mr Carp,"' I said, '"won't you call me Mary?"'

His face brightened a little.

'Then she didn't call you Augustus?' he said.

'She hasn't done so,' I answered, 'as yet.'

'And perhaps she never will,' he said, 'never will.'

'I don't quite see,' I said, 'why you should say that.'

'Perhaps not,' he replied. 'But I do say it.'

'Of course I shouldn't encourage her to,' I said, 'until she had altered her profession.'

'And perhaps she won't,' he said, 'perhaps she won't.'

'Won't what?' I asked.

'Alter her profession.'

'But don't you want her to?' I cried.

'Oh, of course,' he said. 'But they seldom do, you know, unless they marry.'

'Precisely,' I said, 'unless they marry.'

He opened his mouth for a moment, but only breathed through it.

'But you don't mean to tell me,' he said, 'that as Vice-President –?'

'It might be my duty,' I said, 'to sacrifice myself.'

'So much as that?' he said. 'So much as that,

Augustus?'

He covered his eyes for a moment with his gloved hands.

Then he suddenly remembered that he had dropped his umbrella.

'It's here,' I said, 'under my foot.'

'Oh, thank you,' he said, 'thank you.'

Then he held out his hands to me with frank contrition.

'Oh, my dear friend,' he said, 'forgive me for misjudging you. But as your President, I could never permit it.'

'But why not?' I said, trying to release my hands.

'Why, because as President,' he cried, 'it is clearly the sort of sacrifice that I ought to make myself.'

'But I don't see why,' I said, again trying to release myself.

'But don't you see,' he cried, still holding my hands, 'how symbolic it would then become – the marriage of one of the most prominent of our younger ex-actresses with the Anti-Dramatic and Saltatory Union?'

'But she wouldn't be marrying the Union,' I said.

'Not if she married you,' he said, 'who are merely the Vice-President. But if she married me, Augustus, it would be different. It would become the sacrifice of the whole Union.'

'But, my dear Ezekiel,' I said, 'ought you to sacrifice the whole Union without consulting all its members?'

'Oh, but I should,' he said, 'I certainly should, and any that objected I should ask to resign.'

I reflected for a moment. Admirable as was his character, it was in many respects singularly bigoted, while his intelligence, sometimes so brilliant, was at others inferior even to that of his sisters. Since the burial of his parents, too, a couple of years previously, and the consequent augmentation of his own income, I had been conscious in him of a rather unexpected and somewhat disturbing vein of arrogance. I therefore decided, for the present at any rate, that the wisest policy was one of postponement.

'But surely in that case,' I said, 'they should have an opportunity of seeing her.'

'Oh, of course,' he said, 'of course.'

'Before they married her, I mean – as an Union.'

'Oh, certainly,' he said, 'certainly.'

Then his hair parted for a moment, revealing his teeth.

'In fact, I was just going to suggest,' he smiled, 'asking her to one of our meetings.'

'I'll certainly do so,' I said. 'I'll ask her tomorrow.'

'We'll both ask her,' he replied.

'But you won't be there,' I said.

'Yes, I shall,' he answered. 'I shall come with you.'

'But she hasn't invited you,' I said, again trying to free my hands.

'But, my dear Augustus,' he said, gripping them a little tighter, 'surely you don't expect me to wait for that? Does the powerful swimmer refrain from plunging until the drowning victim has asked him to do so, or the hurrying policeman refuse to cut the rope because the would-be suicide has not invited it? Does the fireman hesitate before the smouldering nightgown until the female inside it has shown him her card?'

'Perhaps not,' I said, stepping a pace backwards.

'Certainly not,' he said, following me.

'But on the other hand,' I said, stepping sideways, 'if a powerful swimmer has already plunged, if a hurrying policeman is already there, if a soaring fireman has already stooped –'

'Then that is all the more reason,' he said, also stepping sideways, 'why the hero should be helped as I mean to help you.'

'Well, I can't promise,' I said, 'that she will be willing to receive you.

'Not when she knows,' he asked, 'that I'm the Adult Gripe Water?'

'Well, she might,' I said. 'I'll do my best, of course.'

'Dear Augustus,' he replied, 'I thought you would.'

Then he dropped my hands, now seriously congested, and stooping down, picked up his umbrella.

'And I don't want you to feel,' he added, 'now that I propose to take charge of the work, that your share in it has been unappreciated.'

Then we climbed into the omnibus that was to take us to Camberwell and sat side by side in it in silence, parting as usual, however, with a mutual benediction, though I could not conceal from myself that his attitude had disappointed me. For though it would have been inevitable, and indeed desirable, that subsequent to redemption Miss Moonbeam should have met him, this was scarcely the moment, I felt, for the sudden intrusion of a second deliverer. Nor were the nuptials that he had proposed for her other than profoundly distasteful to me, though a glance at my mirror sufficed to reassure me of their extreme unlikelihood. Nevertheless, I deemed it wise before retiring to bed to send a brief note to Miss

Moonbeam, regretting the pertinacity that would probably result in my being accompanied by Ezekiel, but at the same time indicating that he was not to be dismissed as a wholly valueless acquaintance. 'Nor must you forget,' I concluded, 'that he is at least the President of the great Union that has brought us together.' A difficult letter, it had needed all the tact that I had been able to summon to its composition, and the clock had struck eleven, I remember, before I was able to open my nightgown bag, preparatory to taking out my nightgown.

I was a little pale, therefore, when I arrived at the theatre at six o'clock the next evening, and though fully confident of my ability to control the situation, I was naturally somewhat anxious as to the effect upon Miss Moonbeam of a night's consideration. Had the latent thirst for a higher life, that my person had aroused in her the night before, been submerged again by wicked companions or quickened by my absence? Had she gone to sleep dreaming of the footlights or of an Anti-Dramatic and Saltatory future? And how had the poor child, reared in sin and ignorance, received the letter that I had been obliged to write to her?

Such were the questions that occupied my mind as Ezekiel came hurrying to meet me, and we walked upstairs to the same room in which I had talked with her the night before. For the first moment, too, I was a trifle dazzled both by the brilliance of its illumination and the clamour of conversation that greeted our entrance from the large number of persons whom we found assembled in it. This died down instantly, however, when our names were announced, and as we stood framed for a moment in the doorway, nothing could have been more striking than the effect of our presence upon the actors and actresses huddled before us. I say huddled because, as so often happens when evil-doers are taken by surprise, they had unanimously winced and drawn closer together, while at least two of them had murmured 'Help!' Moreover, it was quite clear that some of them had been drinking, since their wine glasses were still in their hands, and indeed I was almost certain, to my deep consternation, that Miss Moonbeam herself had been one of these.* Her hands were empty, however, when she came forward to greet us, and although Ezekiel had abruptly stiffened, I could not see my way to refuse the manual courtesy, to which she was evidently looking forward.

'Oh, Mr Carp,' she said, 'this is indeed sweet of you. I was beginning to be afraid that you weren't coming.'

'My dear Miss Moonbeam,' I began.

'Mary,' she said.

'My dear Mary,' I said, 'I never break my word.'

'No, no, you wouldn't,' she said, 'and my friends will be so pleased. Let me introduce you to them. This is Mr Augustus Carp.'

I bowed to them gravely.

'And you've brought your friend?' she said.

'The President of our Union,' I said, 'Mr Ezekiel Stool.'

She held out her hand to him.

'I'm sure we shall be great friends,' she said. But he was still staring suspiciously at her colleagues.

* I am now, alas, convinced of this.

'They've been drinking,' he said. 'What have they been drinking?'

'Oh, nothing much,' she said. 'Only my health.'

'Your health?' he repeated.

'Yes, it's my birthday,' she said.

'My dear Miss Mary,' I said. 'Let me congratulate you.'

'Yes, yes, yes,' said Ezekiel. 'But what's the fluid?'

He tilted his face a little, sniffing the air.

'Oh, I see,' said Miss Moonbeam. 'How stupid of me. Reggie, come forward and show them your glass.'

She glanced over her shoulder, and a young man, whom I instantly recognized as the naval officer, then approached us carrying a wine glass filled with a dark, translucent liquid.

'It's delightful stuff,' he said. 'It is really. Won't you taste a little before you begin your sermon?'

But Ezekiel started back, gripping my left elbow, while the hair covering his face extended itself protectively.

'No, no,' he cried. 'Augustus, keep close to me. I don't like the smell of it. Ask him what it's made of.'

I drew myself up a little, facing the naval officer, while Ezekiel clung to my elbow.

'You must pardon us,' I cried, 'but in addition to our connection with the Anti-Dramatic and Saltatory Union, we are also officials – and in this particular work, I hold a higher position than my comrade – we are also officials of the Society for the Prevention of the Strong Drink Traffic. It is therefore not only important to us, since we have been invited to rescue you, to learn whether this also is one of your vices, but doubly necessary that we ourselves should take every possible precaution. You will consequently perceive, I hope, the imperative necessity of our assuring ourselves, before we partake of it, that the composition of the liquor you have proffered us is such as our consciences can approve of.'

'Oh, I'm sure of it,' he said. 'Just smell it.'

'Personally,' I replied, 'I do not object to the smell.'

'And the taste,' he added, 'is even pleasanter.'

'I can quite believe it,' I said. 'But what is it made of?'

'Oh, just fruit,' said Miss Moonbeam. 'It's a sort of fruit squash, you know – a fruit squash, made of fruit.'

Ezekiel advanced a little and put his face against it.

'I prefer the colour,' he said, 'to the smell.'

'Yes, isn't it beautiful?' said the naval officer, and several of the other actors said the same thing.

'But what's it called?' said Ezekiel.

'Portugalade,' said Miss Moonbeam.

'That's because it comes from Portugal,' said the naval officer.

'And one gets used to the smell,' said Ezekiel. 'But why does one drink it out of wine glasses?'

'Oh, but one needn't,' said Miss Moonbeam. 'One can drink it out of tumblers.'

'One just used wine glasses,' said the naval officer, 'because one happened to find them in the cupboard.'

I looked at him piercingly.

'But surely that seems to indicate,' I said, 'that they have been used for other and less innocent beverages.'

He hung his head, and as my glance swept his companions, I observed that most of them hung theirs also.

Then he lifted it again, not without a certain honesty.

'Mr Carp,' he said, 'it's no use deceiving you. And I'm afraid I must confess that I haven't confined myself to such health-giving drinks as this Portugalade.'

'Nor we,' said his companions. 'Nor we.'

'But we hope to do better,' said Miss Moonbeam, 'in the future.'

'Then, ladies and gentlemen,' I said, sipping the Portugalade, which seemed to me exceptionally agreeable, 'I can only implore you – and I speak not only for myself, but for my friend Mr Stool –'

'Of the Adult Gripe Water,' said Ezekiel. 'It was invented by my late father.'

'You don't say so?' said the naval officer.

'Was that what made him late?' asked Miss Moonbeam.

Ezekiel stared at her over the glass of Portugalade, which I had handed on to him before beginning my speech.

'How do you mean late?' he said.

'Wasn't that what you said?' asked Miss Moonbeam.

'Yes, but I meant dead,' said Ezekiel. 'He's been dead some time.'

'You don't mean it?' said the naval officer.

'Yes. It's rather nice,' said Ezekiel.

'I see,' said Miss Moonbeam. 'You didn't get on together?'

'I meant the Portugalade,' said Ezekiel.

'– I can only implore you,' I continued, 'while there's still time – before the craving for stimulants has finally overcome you – to cast them away from you with both hands, to crush them under foot, to leave them for ever.'

I glanced at Ezekiel, who was wiping his mouth.

'And, ladies and gentlemen,' I said, 'why should you hesitate? Have you not here – or had you not there, rather – in the very glass that my friend has just emptied, a drink as genial, as palatable and invigorating as the most debauched of you could desire?'

'We have, we have,' they cried.

'Then, ladies and gentlemen,' I said, 'before we further address you on the evils of the drama, may I not beg of you to make up your minds to drink nothing less healthful than this in the future?'

'You may, you may,' they said.

I turned to Ezekiel.

'Then I'll ask Mr Stool,' I said, 'to inaugurate our second appeal.'

I then stood aside while Ezekiel cleared his throat preparatory to delivering his usual oration, and it was during the course of this that Miss Moonbeam drew me aside and informed me how much she had appreciated my letter.

'I thought it was so dear of you,' she said, 'to let your friend down without seeming to want to do anything of the kind.'

'It was certainly difficult,' I said.

'But you managed it so beautifully,' she said. 'How long do you suppose he will go on speaking?'

'Twenty minutes,' I said. 'This is his half-hour harangue.'

She was looking a little pale, I thought. But she smiled bravely.

'Well, I suppose we deserve it,' she said.

'Oh, undoubtedly,' I replied, 'and he wants you to

attend one of our meetings.'

'What – all of us?' she asked.

'You would all be welcome,' I said.

'And would you be there too?' she asked, pressing my hand.

'Why, of course,' I said, permitting her to continue pressing, 'I am the Vice-President.'

'Yes, I know,' she whispered.

Here Ezekiel paused for a moment and glanced at us keenly. But Miss Moonbeam at once smiled at him and clapped her hands.

'You don't think he's jealous?' she said, as he continued.

'Jealous of what?' I asked.

'Why, of you and me,' she said.

She was pressing my hand again and endeavouring to draw closer to me.

'Well, I'm rather afraid,' I said, 'that he may be.'

'You see,' said Miss Moonbeam, 'if I'm to be rescued by anybody, I should so like it to be by you.'

'Dear Mary,' I said, 'and so it shall, at whatever cost, at whatever sacrifice.'

'Dear Augustus,' she said. 'May I call you Augustus? It sounds so ungrateful to say Mr Carp.'

'Yes, yes,' I said. 'I can quite understand it. But I would rather you suppressed the familiarity in public.'

Then Ezekiel concluded, and after some words from myself, a special meeting of the Union was arranged, at which all our listeners, including Miss Moonbeam, solemnly engaged themselves to be present. It was to take place, we agreed, on the following Sunday week, at the Porter Street Drill Hall in Camberwell, and at Miss

Moonbeam's suggestion, Mr Chrysostom Lorton was
to be invited to say a few words.

'I didn't know you knew him,' I said.

'Nor I do,' she replied. 'But as he's the publisher of
all these beautiful booklets, I thought it would be so
nice if he would just stoop for a moment to mingle with
the sinners for whom they are intended.'

'A splendid idea,' I said, 'and a most intelligent one,
and we'll circularize the churches and chapels, and hold
the meeting at nine in the evening, when the
congregations will be able to be present.'

'Oh, that'll be capital,' she said. 'I should love to see a
congregation.'

'And Ezekiel and myself,' I said, 'will be the chief
speakers.'

She clapped her hands and looked at Ezekiel.

'Oh, Mr Stool,' she cried, 'what a meeting.'

Ezekiel beamed at her.

'Yes, it ought to be worth going to,' he said, 'and I
shall reserve a chair for you next to the President.'

Then she drew me aside again.

'And you must have supper with me first,' she said,
'Just you and me and a few of my friends.'

'My dear Mary,' I said, 'nothing would delight me
more.'

'I feel a whole new world,' she said, 'opening before
me.'

Upon the following Sunday week, therefore, at half-
past seven, I stood outside her house in Bedford Square,
and the next moment I was being led upstairs by a
modestly dressed parlourmaid in a white cap. Clad
myself in a well-fitting morning coat with a hand-knitted

waistcoat and a velveteen tie, I found Miss Moonbeam with her men and women companions eagerly awaiting me in evening dress. About a dozen in all, they included the naval officer and two young men, whom she introduced as her brothers, while there were several females who greeted me with deference, but whose chests, as I pointed out to them, were inadequately covered. They begged my pardon, however, with the not unreasonable excuse that the standards I had set them were not easily reached, and at my urgent request, Miss Moonbeam provided them with napkins to make good the deficiency. This having been attended to, we then went downstairs to a capacious dining-room on the ground floor, where an excellent meal was ushered in with some admirably prepared chicken soup.

Followed by fish, partridges and salad, bowls of stewed fruit and Devonshire cream, it was concluded with a savoury consisting of stuffed eggs mounted on triangular pieces of toast, and I was gratified to observe that, apart from water, the only other beverage was Portugalade. It was again, to my annoyance, however, served in wine glasses, although Miss Moonbeam immediately apologized, pouring out a tumblerful for me with her own hand, just as I was beginning my second partridge. Nor did I find it any less agreeable than upon my first acquaintance with it at the theatre, and indeed I had seldom experienced such a sense of warmth and comfort as it very quickly began to endow me with. Peculiarly attractive to the nostril, it was no less grateful to the tongue, while upon its downward passage, it lent an extraordinary balm to a naturally irritable digestive system.

Nay, it did more, for as it enriched the blood mounting to an always responsive brain, I found myself the vehicle of a delightful flow of new and most valuable ideas. I say valuable, and this was indeed the case, but many of them were also outstandingly humorous, and time after time I was obliged to call for silence so that none of those present might fail to hear them. I was glad to perceive, too, that they met with an instant response both in laughter and rapt attention, and I was soon convinced that, beneath the trappings of guilt, there was a spark of goodness in most of my listeners. Nor had Miss Moonbeam, who kept my tumbler filled, ever appeared to me to be so well worth saving, and when I accidentally upset my fruit, she was solicitude's self as she wiped my waistcoat.

By a second mischance, too, I spilt my coffee, which was served at the supper-table just before we rose; and on this occasion also she was instantly at hand to remove the stains from the upper part of my trousers. Then we rose for grace, which I proposed should be sung, and into the singing of which I threw my whole being; and when I found myself swaying a little, owing to the consequent fatigue, both she and the naval officer kindly supported me. Indeed so acute was the resulting vertigo that I was not only obliged for a moment to sit down, but I found myself only too glad to rely on their aid as we descended the front steps to the waiting vehicles. Glad as I was, however, they both assured me that they were gladder even than I was, while the others assured us, as we glanced across the pavement, that they were gladder even than we were. In fact, we were all glad, and although I had been a little perturbed by the physical disability to which I have referred, I was soon restored by the night air, the motion of the vehicle, and the prospects of the meeting. Moreover, the naval officer had brought with him a large bottle of the Portugalade, and a further draught of this at once completed, and indeed augmented, my sense of well-being.

'Yes, it ought to be grand,' I said, 'a grand meeting, the grandest meeting we've ever had,' and I remember putting my head out of the right-hand window and inviting the passers-by to come and join us.

'Yes, there's no doubt of it,' I said, 'it'll be a grand meeting, a grand, grand meeting, grander and grander.'

'As grand as grand,' said the naval officer.

'Yes, and grander than that,' I said, 'ever so grand.'

Then I started a hymn just to clear my chest again, and finding, to my satisfaction, that it was surprisingly supple, I led my companions through chorus after chorus of a brisk but devotional character. Indeed we were in the middle of one when we arrived at the Drill Hall, and so intent had I become on the music that I unfortunately tripped as I alighted upon the pavement and struck my abdomen rather violently. Two of Miss Moonbeam's brothers, however, who were waiting to receive us, at once readjusted me upon my legs, while the naval officer came to their assistance in conducting me to my chair upon the platform.

Nor had I been in error in foreseeing an audience that filled the hall to its utmost capacity, Miss Moonbeam herself and several of her companions being audibly recognized on their way to their seats. Many of our members, too, in different parts of the hall, were standing on their feet, I noticed, to give me a personal welcome; and no sooner had I hailed these in affectionate terms than others took their places to be hailed in turn. So prolonged, in fact, did these greetings become, and to such a pitch of heartiness did they climb, that Ezekiel's own arrival upon the platform, accompanied by Mr Chrysostom Lorton, was scarcely noticed.

That was probably the reason, I inferred, why his expression was almost less pleasant than I had ever known it, and why he obviously resented the attentions of Miss Moonbeam's brothers, who were still standing, one on each side of me. Mr Chrysostom, too, seemed curiously distant, I thought, as I swung round and clasped his hand, although I assured him, in tones that rang through the hall, of my intense delight at his presence.

'Simply overwhelmed,' I said, 'simply overwhelmed, Mr Chrysostom. Let me introduce you to Miss Moonbeam. Miss Moonbeam, Mr Chrysostom Lorton. Mr Chrysostom Lorton, Miss Moonbeam.'

Then I turned to the audience with a great shout.

'Three cheers,' I cried, 'for Mr Chrysostom Lorton. Hip– hip –'

But Ezekiel held up his hand.

'I propose to open this meeting,' he said, 'with prayer.'

For a moment I was staggered. Indeed I almost fell down. It was the directest insult I had ever received. And it was not only an insult to myself, but to Mr Chrysostom, who was deprived of his cheers.

'Oh, how dare you?' I cried. 'How dare you, Ezekiel? Oh, Mr Chrysostom, how dare he? Hip, hip, I say – Hip, hip,' but the audience remained silent and evidently confused. In fact, the effect upon them of Ezekiel's proposal must have been exasperating in the extreme, since they had all opened their mouths and protruded their upper lips preparatory to cheering, as I had suggested. They had then been obliged, just as they had taken their breaths, to retract their upper lips again and close their mouths, and were naturally reluctant, in spite of my further exhortation, to resume a process once frustrated. Nevertheless, many of them did so, although they failed in its final consummation, with the lamentable result that they resembled nothing so much as goldfish breathing in a bowl.

'Goldfish,' I cried. 'That's what they are. Poor lost goldfish, without a shepherd. Oh, Ezekiel, Ezekiel Stool! How could you do such a thing as that?'

With incredible determination, however, he was already on his knees and in the second paragraph of his supplication; and it was only after I had shaken him several times that he sprang to his feet with a sort of yelp.

'Oh, Ezekiel,' I said, 'what a horrible noise.'

'Leave me alone,' he snarled. 'Can't you see I'm busy?'

'Horrible noise,' I said, 'horrible, horrible. Isn't it a horrible noise, Mr Chrysostom?'

Then I turned to the audience again.

'Let's say it all together,' I said. 'One, two, three, horrible noise. That's better. Now let's say it again. One, two –'

Then I stopped abruptly, for as I advanced to the brink of the platform, with Miss Moonbeam's brothers at my elbows, I suddenly became aware of a solitary grey eye regarding me objectionably from the front row. Its fellow was of glass, and the face that contained them, with its high cheek-bones and gaunt cheeks, was that of none other than Mr Archibald Maidstone, the show-room manager whom I had succeeded.

For a moment I could scarcely believe it. But hardly had I recovered myself than I found myself in his arms, with Miss Moonbeam's brothers left upon the plat-form, each holding a moiety of the tail of my coat.'

'Well, laddie,' he said, 'it's your turn now.'

I endeavoured to push myself away from him.

'Take him away,' I shouted. 'Take that man away. Where's Mr Chrysostom? Where's Miss Moonbeam?'

The tumult in the hall was now indescribable. Glasses of water were on every side of me. But I thrust them all aside and shouted to the naval officer to bring me the bottle that he had placed upon the table.

'The bottle,' I cried. 'Bring me the bottle. Never mind the glass. Give me the bottle.'

But the naval officer, evidently at his request, had handed the bottle to Mr Chrysostom. I saw him examine it through his spectacles in his usual pompous and deliberate fashion and then, with a heightened colour and protuberant eyes, exhibit it to Ezekiel and the members of the committee.

'Disgraceful,' he said, 'perfectly disgraceful. The fellow's drunk, I say. Just look at that. Vintage Port, and he's been drinking it out of a tumbler. Perfectly disgraceful. Show me the way out.'

I rose to my feet and caught sight of Miss Moonbeam's brothers.

'Give me that bottle,' I cried. 'Give me the tails of my

coat. Who says I'm drunk? Where's the Portugalade? Take that man away. Where's Miss Moonbeam?'

'But he's my father,' she said.

I tried to stare at her. But her face kept advancing and retreating.

'Stand still, woman,' I cried. 'But his name's Maidstone.'

'So's mine,' she said, 'when I'm not acting.'

I snatched at her wrist, but it proved to be my own.

'Do you mean to say,' I asked, 'that you're Mary Maidstone?'

'Polly Maidstone,' she said. 'Don't you remember? The same Polly that made a face at you.'

I sank to the floor for a moment, but rose on my hands again.

'Throw her out,' I yelled. 'Throw that woman out.'

She looked at Ezekiel.

'Hadn't we better take him home?' she asked.

'But I haven't made my speech,' I said, 'speech to the meeting.'

Ezekiel stared at me with incredible bitterness.

'There isn't a meeting left,' he said, 'to make a speech to.'

I pointed at the clocks. They were all at half-past nine.

'But we've hardly begun,' I said. 'Where's the platform?'

Mr Maidstone bent over me –*

*See conclusion of Chapter 8

Chapter Seventeen

Profound depression subsequent to port-poisoning. An iniquitous plot and its consequences. Insubordination of Miss Botterill. I retire from the firm of Mr Chrysostom Lorton. A crushing rejoinder and its repetition. Second journey to Enfield. Transformation of Mrs Chrysostom's boudoir. Unexpected repentance of Mrs Chrysostom. Unfortunate results of this for myself. Fruitless termination of interview.

Such was the cross that had suddenly been imposed upon me – a cross so gigantic and of such a character that only the most prolonged and assiduous training could have enabled me to hear it. Indeed, for some little time it seemed only too likely that it would prove too crushing even for me; and had not Nature intervened with a period of merciful unconsciousness, this would almost certainly have been the case. Fortunately I arrived home, however, as my father has assured me, in a deep though stertorous slumber, and did not awake until nearly eleven o'clock on the following Monday morning. There was thus accorded me an opportunity for the recuperation of those vital reserves that would even then, as I slowly began to realize, be desperately hard put to it to give me adequate support.

I say slowly because, when I first woke, my physical nausea was so great that I was totally unable to form a clear judgement upon the events of the previous evening. Nor was my mother, never a fluent speaker, more communicative than usual. I had been brought home, she said, by two young gentlemen, whose names she did not know, and a doctor had been called in, at my father's request, who had made a diagnosis with which my father disagreed. Indeed my father, I gathered, had been considerably upset, and had spent a restless night in consequence, and my mother had been obliged on three separate occasions to prepare him a cup of malted milk. Shen then awaited my orders for breakfast. But this was a meal that I was compelled to omit. And it was only after she had left me that my memory began to recover itself and to lay its sombre offerings at the feet of my judgement. Then I rang the bell again and inquired of my mother the exact terms of the doctor's diagnosis. But she shook her head and referred me to my father, who would be able to tell me, she said, when he returned from business.

'Not that it much matters,' she added, 'for you'd be sure to disagree with it.'

'I certainly should,' I replied, 'and I certainly shall. I was poisoned – deliberately poisoned – by the wicked woman with whom I had my supper.'

'An actress, I believe,' said my mother.

'Whom I was prepared to save,' I said, 'from a deserved perdition.'

My mother was silent for a moment.

'Is that all?' she said.

'How do you mean, all?' I asked.

'I mean, may I go now?'

'Oh, yes, yes,' I said. 'Shut the door quietly, please; and I should like my shaving water in about an hour.'

Then I lay back quietly, closing my eyes in pain and rehearsing such speeches as would be necessary to put both Mr Chrysostom Lorton and Ezekiel Stool in the full possession of the facts of the case. It would also be essential, I foresaw, to call a further special meeting of the Anti-Dramatic and Saltatory Union and to make a point of addressing, at the earliest opportunity, the Society for the Prevention of the Strong Drink Traffic. It would be equally important, too, in my capacity of gap-filler, to prepare an explanatory petition for use at the local prayer-meetings, the majority of which had contributed members to last night's audience in the Porter Street Drill Hall. Yes, it was all coming back to me in its devilish ingenuity (for it had evidently been a plot on the part of Mr Maidstone's daughter), and she might depend upon it that if legal redress were possible, it should be extracted from her to the last farthing.

But was it possible? The more I considered it, the more doubtful I became. And even were it possible, would it be expedient? The condition of my head forbade an immediate answer. Indeed I was now the subject of a thirst so overwhelming that without pausing to summon my mother, I was obliged to quench it from the various receptacles within easy reach upon my wash-hand stand. I was profoundly shocked, too, by the aspect of my countenance, as this was disclosed to me by my looking-glass; and accustomed as I was to a frequently concealed tongue, I had never before seen it so deeply obscured. Even after I had shaved and dressed, indeed, I was a little doubtful as to whether I should be able to complete the journey to town. But I was determined if possible not only to make the attempt, but to perform my usual afternoon duties. After a cup of tea therefore, and a fragment of dried herring, I ventured into the street and mounted an omnibus, arriving in Paternoster Row at about two o'clock to find Miss Botterill in charge of the show-room.

'Good afternoon,' I said. 'I have been the victim of a dastardly plot, or I should have been in my place this morning as usual.'

'Good afternoon,' she replied, 'and please, Mr Chrysostom said, would you go up to his room as soon as you arrived.'

'Certainly,' I said, 'and when I come down, Miss Botterill, I should like to see that counter looking a little tidier.'

Miss Botterill hesitated.

'I'm just rearranging it,' she said. 'I propose in future to have it less crowded.'

I stared at her.

'You propose what?' I asked.

'I propose in future,' she said, 'to have a bowl of flowers upon it and merely a very few of our latest books.'

Depleted as I felt, I yet retained command of myself.

'But, my dear Miss Botterill,' I said, 'permit me to remind you that your duty is to obey and not propose. You will therefore kindly restore the counter to its previous appearance and remember in future that you are not show-room manager.'

'But I am,' she said.

She continued her rearranging.

Deprived of breath, I could only stand and watch her.

Then I leapt forward and gripped her shoulder.

'Oh, how dare you?' I cried. 'How dare you, woman?'

She began to scream. But I declined to let her go until several of the clerks had emerged from the correspondence room. Then I flung her from me heavily, turned upon my heel, and instantly proceeded to Mr Chrysostom's office. He was standing at the door.

'What's all this screaming?' he said.

'I regret to say,' I replied, 'that Miss Botterill has been insubordinate.'

'Insubordinate?' he said. 'And to whom, please?'

'To myself,' I replied, 'as your representative.'

'Then kindly understand,' he said, 'kindly understand, sir, that after last night –'

I waved my hand.

'One moment,' I said. 'It is to explain about last night that I have managed to force myself to come and see you.'

He distended his cheeks.

'Then you could have spared yourself the trouble,' he said. 'I don't want to see your face again.'

'But, my dear sir,' I said.

'I'm not your dear sir,' he shouted. 'I'm not your dear anything. I've no further use for you.'

But I held up my hand again.

'I must beg you to control yourself,' I said, 'until this unfortunate mishap has been fully explained to you.

'Mishap?' he said. 'Do you call it a mishap, sir, to invite your employer to a religious gathering and leave him to be received by a thing like a stunted gorilla, because you're too drunk to stand by yourself?'

'But, my dear sir,' I began.

'Don't say that again,' he said. 'Don't say anything again. I don't want to hear it. You were drunk, sir. You

201

were damnably drunk. You were so drunk that you fell off the platform.'

Involuntarily I winced, as who would not have done? But once more I held up my hand.

'Mr Lorton,' I said, 'you have forgotten who I am, or such words could never have escaped you. And I was neither drunk, nor would have such a thing have been possible. I was merely suffering from deliberate port-poisoning.'

If anything, however, he became more violent.

'Port-poisoning?' he bawled. 'What's port-poisoning? Port isn't poison, sir. I drink it myself. In fact, I was obliged, sir, to drink some of your own – an excellent port, sir, that probably saved my life.'

'I regret to hear it,' I said. 'But allow me to point out to you that the fluid you mention was not my own, and that I had been informed by its donors that it was a species of fruit squash, imported from Portugal and known as Portugalade.'

'But, good God, sir, there's no such thing.'

'Precisely,' I replied. 'That's my point.'

'Your point?' he cried. 'What do you mean by your point?'

'Why, that I was refreshed,' I said, 'and subsequently disabled by a beverage that has no existence.'

'Then you're a fool,' he said. 'You're either a knave, sir – a drunken knave – or a fool.'

'Then am I to understand,' I said, 'that I am no longer show-room manager?'

'You're no longer anything,' he said, 'in any business of mine.'

I leaned against the wall.

'And you call yourself a Xtian gentleman?' I said.

'I certainly do,' he said, 'and I thank God for it.'

Then I stood erect again, dashing the tears from my eyes. He pulled out his handkerchief.

'Don't wet me,' he said.

'It was inadvertent,' I said.

'I'm glad to hear it,' he replied.

'And I apologize,' I said, 'to the moisture.'

For a moment he gaped at me, and little wonder. It was perhaps the crushingest remark in human history.

'I apologize,' I said, 'to the moisture.'

Yes, it must have cut him to the quick.

It was so crushing, indeed, that I repeated it to Miss Botterill.

'Miss Botterill,' I said, 'I am leaving.'

'Yes, I know,' she said. 'I knew before you came.'

'May I beg,' I replied, 'that you won't interrupt me.'

She was silent, and I continued.

'And one of my tears,' I said, 'fell on Mr Chrysostom.'

'Oh dear,' she said. 'Poor Mr Chrysostom.'

'So I apologized,' I said.

'Quite right,' she said.

'But not to Mr Chrysostom,' I said. 'I apologized to the moisture.'

'To the moisture?' she said. 'What moisture?'

'Why, to the moisture,' I explained, 'of the tear.'

She stared at me with her mouth open.

'But what was the good of that?' she asked. 'The moisture couldn't hear you.'

'No. It couldn't hear me,' I said, 'it couldn't hear me, Miss Botterill. But don't you see that by apologizing to the moisture, I was conveying to Mr Chrysostom, in the most trenchant way possible, my own opinion of his character.'

'No, I don't,' said Miss Botterill. 'I don't see it at all.'

'Then I'll explain it,' I said, 'over again.'

Just at that moment, however, a customer entered the show-room, and although I waited for several minutes, another customer entered the show-room just as the first was departing. I therefore decided to leave the premises, spurning them, as I did so, with my right foot, and it was not until I had already turned into Ludgate Hill that I suddenly remembered my unused weapon. Mrs Chrysostom Lorton – I had utterly forgotten her. Indeed I had never seen her since my first interview. But she had always been there, of course – there in the background – ready to be used in an emergency like this. I stopped short. Yes, I had forgotten her. But to have remembered her was to act at once. For there could be no doubt about it. It would be wholly impossible for her to afford to sit still and have me dismissed. I therefore advanced to the kerbstone and hailed an omnibus, and within half an hour of conceiving the idea was in a third-class carriage leaving Liverpool Street Station upon my second visit to Enfield. Depressed as I was, too, both physically and mentally, in spite of my crushing rejoinder to Mr Chrysostom, my spirits perceptibly rose as I neared my destination, stimulated by the memory of my previous triumph. For though a good many years had now elapsed since I last stood in that lascivious boudoir, Time had not dimmed the spiritual victory that it had been my privilege to gain there.

It was with an eye, therefore, comparatively clear that I

once more approached Paternoster Towers and with a hand almost steady that I again knocked at its front door. Nor was the strange parlourmaid that received my card and presently conducted me to Mrs Chrysostom's room appreciably less respectful in her demeanour than the gentle domestic that had first received me. But the room itself, apart from its floor, which was now almost lecherous in its degree of polish, was so transformed that for several moments I could scarcely believe myself in the same apartment. Gone was the French-looking writing-table with its reflected legs. Gone was the nude huntress with the splinter in her calf. Gone was the oval mirror with its indelicate Cupids. Gone even was the photograph signed Your aff. Chrysostom. Nay, gone was the very couch with its sensuous cushions, and in its place stood a low divan, padded it was true, and not uncomfortably, but cushioned and draped with the sombrest purple.

There hung upon the walls, too, what were apparently lists of commandments, engraved upon parchment in foreign characters, while in each angle of the room stood a sort of shrine containing an alabaster image and an electric candle. Moreover, although it was still daylight, the curtains were drawn; a casket of incense swung from the ceiling; and between the lists of commandments hung various religious implements, phylacteries, wands, and sacrificial knives.

Profound, and indeed disturbing, however, as were the changes in the room, those in Mrs Chrysostom were even more remarkable, although in actual appearance she had altered very little since I had last been obliged to interview her. It was just conceivable, in fact, that for less

disciplined eyes she might still have retained a certain
attraction, not unenhanced by the severity of her gown
and the sober arrangement of her hair. Parted at the side,
this now fell over her brow in a single yellowish-coloured
wave, while her dark dress – it was still clinging, I noticed
– was unadorned in every respect. Her whole mien, too,
was entirely different, and as she drooped, as it were, into
the room, she extended her hand to me with a sort of
grave surprise, as if I had been some stranger whom she
had never seen.

'How do you do?' she said, sinking upon the divan.
'This is my little temple. Won't you sit down?'

I glanced about me.

'I can't offer you a chair,' she said. 'But you'll find
my prayer-mat just behind you.'

Just as I put my heel upon it, however, it began to
slip, and leaning over, she put her finger upon it.

'Let me hold it,' she said, 'while you lower yourself. I
once had a visitor who lost two of his trouser-buttons.'

'It was myself,' I said.

She looked at me steadfastly.

'But surely,' she said, 'I haven't seen you before?'

I bowed to her gravely.

'You certainly have,' I said.

She lifted her eyebrows a little.

'But can that be possible?' she asked.

'It is not only possible,' I said, 'but it actually
happened.'

Her tapering fore-finger touched my knee.

'Then forgive me,' she said, 'but, if I may venture to
say so, hasn't Time been exceedingly kind to you?'

I stared at her.

'I don't quite follow,' I said.

'No, of course not,' she said, 'your modesty would forbid it. But I can scarcely conceive that, if such had not been the case, I should have failed to remember you.'

'Of course I have matured,' I said.

She nodded imperceptibly.

'That is what I meant,' she said. 'I think you must have.'

'But it is rather about the future,' I said, 'than the past that I have been obliged to call upon you this afternoon.'

Her eyes became dreamy, although they were still fixed upon me.

'Ah, the future,' she said, 'the unknown future.'

'And you will be sorry to hear,' I said, 'that owing to a misunderstanding, Mr Chrysostom has requested me to leave.'

'Do you mean my husband?' she asked.

'Why, of course,' I replied.

'Dear Chrysostom,' she said. 'This is some of his hair.'

She showed me a small locket containing the article mentioned.

'I am compelled to remind you,' I said, 'that you were not always so affectionate.'

'No, that's true,' she said, 'that's very true. But happily I also have matured.'

I stared at her again, a trifle uneasily.

'Then perhaps you have forgotten,' I said, 'your friend Septimus?'

'Completely,' she said. 'Was there one?'

Had the floor been less slippery, I should have risen to my feet.

'Mr Septimus Lorton,' I said, 'your husband's brother.'

'You mean the one,' she said, 'that's just passed on?'

'Passed on?' I replied. 'Where to?'

She waved her hands towards several of the shrines.

'Ah, if we but knew,' she said, 'if we but knew, Mr Carp.'

'But do you mean to tell me,' I cried, 'that he's defunct?'

'Run over,' she said, 'last week.'

For a moment, I must confess, I was a little taken aback.

'But that doesn't alter the fact,' I said, 'that he was your lover.'

'Very likely not,' she said. 'I don't remember. But I daresay you're right. There have been so many.'

'But do you mean to say,' I asked, 'that there has been more than one?'

'Oh far, far more than one,' she said.

I began to rise again, and she put her finger on the mat.

'Let me hold it,' she said, 'while you get up.'

This she did, and after a certain amount of difficulty, I once more towered above her.

'But your husband?' I said. 'Does your husband know?'

'Everything,' she said. 'In fact, all.'

I took a deep breath, followed by another.

'But what did he say?' I asked at last.

She closed her eyes for a moment.

'I'm afraid I oughtn't to tell you,' she said. 'You see, since then I've embraced religion.'

'Religion?' I said. 'What religion?'

'Every religion,' she said. 'I've embraced them all.'

'But how could you do that?' I asked.

'Oh, there was no difficulty,' she said. 'It has always been natural to me to embrace.'

I glanced round the room.

'But certain religions,' I said, 'involve the slaughter of human beings.'

'Yes, I know,' she said. 'I've included them. That's why those knives are hanging on the wall.'

'But surely you don't practise them?' I said.

'No, they're cancelled out,' she said, 'by the religions that forbid the taking of life.'

'But it seems to me,' I said, 'that, at that rate, all your religions cancel each other out.'

'Yes,' she replied. 'That's what it often seems to me.'

'But then you haven't a religion at all?'

'Well, I sometimes doubt it,' she said. 'I often wonder if I did the right thing in embracing them.'

It was not to discuss her religion, however, that I had journeyed to Enfield, as I was now somewhat tartly obliged to remind her.

'And you seem to be forgetting,' I added, 'that I've just been dismissed from the employment you were compelled to find me.'

'Yes, I know,' she said. 'But why should I remember it?'

'Because you might prefer,' I said, 'to get the decision altered.'

She lifted her eyes to me.

'Prefer it to what?' she inquired.

'Why, to permitting your husband,' I said, 'to hear from my lips the story of your relations with his brother Septimus.'

'Oh, but I don't mind that,' she said, 'now that I've repented. And besides, as I told you, I'd forgotten all about it.'

With growing uneasiness, I took another deep breath.

'But surely you're not prepared,' I said, 'to let me tell him?'

'On the contrary,' she said, 'I should welcome it, though I doubt if it would interest him after all the others.'

I began to sway a little.

'But, my dear Mrs Chrysostom,' I said, 'if you behave like that, I shall remain dismissed.'

'But surely, Mr Carp,' she answered, 'and I can see you're a good man, it's the only behaviour consistent with repentance.'

I pulled out my handkerchief and wiped my forehead.

'Then you wouldn't speak a word,' I asked, 'on my behalf?'

She shook her head gently.

'It is one of my rules,' she said, 'never to interfere with dear Chrysostom's business.'

I glanced round the room again. My hat was on one of the shrines.

'And you haven't yet told me,' she said, 'that you're glad I've repented.'

'Oh, I am,' I said. 'I am glad.'

'Then I mustn't detain you,' she said. 'Mind the polish.'

Chapter Eighteen

*Physical reaction following my interview with Mrs Chrysostom.
Reception of a wreath from the Maidstones. Moving excerpt
from Simeon's diary. I decide to marry one of Ezekiel's sisters.
Interview with Ezekiel and his deplorable language. Tact is
selected to become my bride. Tragic return to Mon Repos. I fall
unconscious, parallel to my father.*

Glad as I was, however, and indeed, as a Xtian gentleman, glad as I was compelled to be that Mrs
Chrysostom had repented, it was nevertheless a
penitence that in respect of myself was little short of
disastrous. And even now it is with the utmost difficulty
that I can look back upon the weeks that followed.
Deprived of my living; already nearing thirty; and the
subject, as I soon found, of the grossest misjudgement
– such was my prostration that for nearly three weeks, I
was confined to my bedroom, if not to my bed. For two
or three days, in fact, I doubted if I could recover, a
doubt that was shared by my dear father; while a small
wreath, sent by the Maidstones, was actually delivered
at the house. Whether this was despatched under
a misapprehension; whether it was the symbol of a
genuine contrition; or whether it was merely a sop to an
uneasy conscience, will probably never be determined.
And I refrained from acknowledging it until I had come
to a decision as to the possibilities of legal action. After
a prolonged interview, however, with Mr Balfour Whey,

and in view of my poor father's unhappy experiences, it was regretfully decided that the British judiciary was too uncertain to be relied upon; and in a brief sentence, therefore, at the beginning of a letter, I informed Miss Maidstone of its safe arrival. The remainder of the letter, of which I still have a copy, was perhaps the severest exposure of a female character that has ever been penned, with the possible exception of certain passages in the Book of Revelation.

Another document, of which I have a copy, and which was also indited by me, while in bed, was rendered necessary by the widespread local confusion between acute port-poisoning and ordinary inebriation – a confusion accentuated, and indeed never wholly dispersed, owing to the despicable attitude of Mr Chrysostom. Thanks to the generosity, however, of my kind friend Simeon Whey, who had not been present at the meeting, I was enabled to print several hundreds of these for personal and vicarious distribution, agents being posted, upon the following Sunday, at the doors of St Nicholas, Newington Butts, and, during the ensuing week, at the exits and entrances of all my habitual haunts of prayer. In so far as I knew their addresses, too, the pamphlet was sent by post to the members of the *A.D.S.U.* and *S. P. S. D. T.*, and to such other persons as might reasonably have been presumed to have been present at the Porter Street Drill Hall.

For the most part, however, I lay for long hours either comatose or actually asleep, all my meals being brought to my bedside and consumed in a semi-recumbent posture. Nor, had they come, should I have been able to receive visitors, although I made an

The Rev. Simeon Whey from a photograph in my possession

exception in favour of Simeon Whey, who bicycled from Balham every Wednesday and Saturday, not only as a friend, but also as a clergyman. Indeed in many ways I found his ministrations more soothing than those of my father, who had transferred both his Bible and the harmonium from the parlour downstairs to my bedroom. His voice, however, though still very powerful, was much more uncertain than it used to be, and I was usually obliged, after about three-quarters of an hour, to ask him to desist from further vocalization.

So the days passed, one after another, and each a little longer than the one before; and although I endeavoured to summon, and I trust not unsuccessfully, the whole of my accumulated spiritual reserves, it was only by an effort that many would have judged superhuman that I began almost imperceptibly to regain my strength. Indeed, to at least one observer the spectacle I was now presenting was so fractionally short of a miracle that, as he wrote in his diary (for it was none other than Simeon), it 'will never cease to be an inspiration to me'. But let me quote the whole passage, written after I had been in bed for about a fortnight.

'Today,' he wrote, 'I have again visited my poor friend, Augustus Carp, who is still laid aside on the bed of complete exhaustion as the result of the deception that I have already described; and more than ever, as I perceived him lying there, did I regret my absence from the meeting in question. Visibly flushed, although this may perhaps have been due to the imperfect absorption of a recent meal, his eyes were focused upon a point in the ceiling with an almost tragic intensity, and the mute endurance with which he awaits the future will never cease to be an inspiration to me. Nor will he fail, as it seems to me, to need it. For with his chief means of sustenance rent away from him, it will probably become obligatory for him, as he has faintly whispered to me, to marry one of the sisters of Ezekiel Stool.'

That is the whole passage, and I have thought well to include it not only as an encouragement to the afflicted but also as an indication of the poignant decision to which I was now slowly being forced, for, as I had instantly feared on leaving Mrs Chrysostom, and as I had since perceived, alas, only too distinctly, I was face to face with just such a catastrophe as marriage with a Stool had been kept in reserve for. Nor had I been able to discern, bitterly though I had sought for it, any practicable alternative – or none that would preserve me from the personal indignity of applying for fresh employment without adequate references.

Any such employment, too, even if I were to obtain it, would inevitably be associated with a loss of income that would seriously cripple me in those fuller religious duties for which I was so evidently being prepared. For this at any rate had become abundantly clear to me – and indeed it was the sheet anchor by which I clung to life – that I could not but emerge from such an abyss of suffering enormously the richer in strength of character. More than ever, therefore, would it be desirable in future not only that I should be immune from financial anxiety but that I should have at my disposal a larger amount of leisure for my more sacred avocations. Indeed, if this were possible, I felt that henceforward I should be entirely freed from the necessity for money-making, and thereby liberated for the completer uplifting of all with whom I might be brought into contact.

Such, then, were the conclusions to which I had been driven, and which I would already have communicated to Ezekiel, had the latter visited me on what Simeon has so well described as the bed of complete exhaustion. Since I had been carried from the meeting, however, to Miss Maidstone's vehicle – it was her two brothers who had borne me home – I had neither looked upon Ezekiel's face nor received a message from his lips; and this in spite of the fact that I had sent him six of my pamphlets for his own use and that of his sisters. I therefore decided, when I had accumulated sufficient strength – and this was not for another fortnight — to visit him in my own person, though naturally I did so with considerable reluctance.

Nor can I say that I was agreeably impressed either by his reception of me or his subsequent attitude, in which I could not but detect a good deal of that arrogance lately so manifest in his character. It was quite clear, however, that the subject of my errand did not take him by surprise, and indeed he assured me, almost at once, that he had been expecting it for some days. He then remained silent with his back to the fire and continued to stare at me rather offensively.

'Do you mind,' I said, 'if I sit down?'

'Not at all,' he replied. 'You can do as you please.'

I therefore did so, but so distant was his manner that it was difficult to reconcile it, as I immediately pointed out to him, either with his duty as a Xtian or his privileges as an host.

'In fact, you appear to have forgotten,' I said, 'though I pray I may be wrong, that I was once the means of saving your life.'

He breathed unpleasantly through his right nostril.

'Very possibly,' he said. 'But to what end? To the deliberate ruination of the *A.D.S.U.* and all my prospects of marrying Miss Moonbeam.'

'But, my dear Ezekiel,' I began.

He interrupted me coldly.

'I must beg you in future,' he said, 'to call me Mr Stool.'

I stared at him.

'Call you Mr Stool,' I gasped, 'after all these years of impassioned friendship?'

He waved his hand.

'I repudiate them,' he said. 'I repudiate them in their entirety.'

I drew myself up to a right angle with my lap.

'But, Mr Stool,' I said, 'surely you must realize the enormous magnitude of your escape?'

'Escape?' he said. 'Escape from what?'

'Why, from the wickedness,' I replied, 'that I have been the means of revealing to you in the bottomless depths of Miss Moonbeam's heart.'

He blew away the hair from before his lips.

'But I shouldn't have been marrying her wickedness,' he said. 'I should have been marrying herself.'

'Herself?' I cried. 'But you don't mean to tell me that you were attached to her as a female?'

'Yes, I do,' he said. 'Intensely. I was intensely attached to her as a female.'

'But then, if you had married her,' I said, 'it wouldn't have been a sacrifice.'

'How do you know?' he said. 'How do you know it

217

wouldn't?'

'Why, because you'd have liked it,' I said. 'You'd have liked marrying her.'

'Well, of course,' he replied. 'And some people like sacrificing.'

'But, my dear Mr Stool,' I began, 'now that her wickedness has been revealed to you –'

'I don't care a damn,' he said, 'about her wickedness.'

Had I been stronger, I should have leapt to my feet.

'You don't care a what?' I asked.

'A damn,' he said.

'A damn?' I cried.

'Yes, a damn,' he repeated.

I leaned back, closing my eyes.

'Yes, and I've said worse things.'

I opened them again.

'I've said bally and hell and blow.'

He paused for a moment.

'And I've said blast. That's the sort of man, Mr Carp, that you've turned me into.'

'But, my dear Mr Stool,' I said, 'as your future brother-in-law –'

'Yes. But I'm not at all sure,' he said, 'that you will be.'

Had I been erect, I should certainly have fallen. And indeed, as it was, I barely retained consciousness.

'But, Ezekiel,' I cried, 'Mr Stool, surely you haven't forgotten your word of honour.'

'No, I haven't,' he said. 'I haven't. But then you were a man without moral stain.'

'And am I not now?' I asked. 'Am I not now, Mr Stool? Is the victim soiled by the criminal's guilt? Is the pioneer, drawn from the morass, responsible for his

The twin sisters of Ezekiel Stool. The right
hand one became my wife

temporary discoloration?'

He was silent for a moment, but in so far as it was visible, his expression was far from reassuring. Then he rang the bell, and Tact entered the room. She was the less attractive of the twins.

'That's the one,' he said. 'I made them draw lots. But you can only marry her on one condition – that you sign an agreement to live north of the Thames and make a home for her four sisters.'

He tilted his chin a little and put his hands in his pockets. A distant dog barked three times. With a supreme effort I clung to my senses.

'Do you mean all,' I whispered, 'including Faith?'

Faith was the least attractive of the three triplets.

'All or none,' he said.

He pulled out his watch.

I could hear it ticking.

'Why did you do that?' I asked.

'I'm giving you a minute,' he said, 'in which to decide.'

Faint though I was, I staggered to my feet.

'Then as a Xtian,' I said, 'no less than a gentleman –'

'Thirty seconds,' he said.

'I'll take her.'

He replaced his watch, and I took Tact's hand. All the female Stools have poor circulations.

'So we'll be getting married,' I said, 'in due course.'

'Yes,' she said. 'That'll be very nice.'

Then her four sisters, who had evidently been waiting outside, came and shook hands with me with expressions of delight, and Ezekiel informed me that his solicitor would be in attendance the next morning.

I bowed a little stiffly.

'I shall be here,' I said, and Ezekiel replied that he had no doubt of it.

Then I shook hands again with Tact and her sisters, bidding them goodbye for the present; and they bade me goodbye, also for the present, adding that they would be seeing me tomorrow.

'Yes, tomorrow,' I said. 'I'll be seeing you tomorrow.'

'Then we'll say goodbye,' they said, 'till tomorrow.'

'Yes, till tomorrow, I said, 'tomorrow morning.'

'Then we'll say goodbye,' they said, 'till tomorrow morning.'

Nor did I fail to keep the appointment, though little did I dream, as I groped for the door, that not even yet had I been called upon to face the ultimate temperature of my refining fire. For hardly had I arrived, somewhat fresher than I expected, at the garden gate of Mon Repos when there staggered up to it a railway omnibus, congested to the limit of its legal capacity. Deformed with luggage and distended with females, a single glance was sufficient to paralyse me, though less on my own account than on that of my father, who now stood transfixed on the doorstep. Then he gave a small cry of the extremest pathos, and as my mother's eight sisters descended to the pavement, he fell forward upon the garden path, never to rise again.

But it was too much even for me, shaken as I had been to my very foundations, and turning my back and covering my eyes from that hurrying, Welsh-speaking female flood, I fell forward parallel to my father, though with my head in the opposite direction.

Chapter Nineteen

Commencement of my life's afternoon. My father's eight sisters-in-law return to Wales. Astounding attitude of my mother. Physical effect thereof on myself. I move to Stoke Newington. Further parochial activities. Simeon Whey obtains a living. I move to Hornsey and become a Churchwarden. Complete decline of Ezekiel Stool. Birth of my son. A happy augury.

Yes, I fell down; Nature could stand no more; and a discerning Providence, relenting at last, mercifully granted me a moment's oblivion while my mother's eight sisters swept over me. But I was never to be the same man again; and I have always regarded that unconscious moment as definitely conducting me into what has happily proved the long afternoon of my life. For it must not be thought that I am repining, or that, looking back over the intervening years, I am anything but grateful for that final ordeal, through which my character was required to pass. On the contrary – *post tenebras lux* * – as I have often remarked to my wife and her sisters, I can only thank Heaven that I was considered worthy of so prolonged and fierce a discipline.

Nor do I propose, as I now turn, in this the final chapter of my book, to the quiet contemplation of the fruitful activities with which my later life has been concerned – nor do I propose, I say, to linger unduly over the tragic incidents just recorded. Defeated in

*After darkness light.

their object by what I have since been informed was the rupture of an important cerebral artery, my father's eight murderesses – for such, in fact, they were – were obliged to return again to Llanpwhllanpwh, though not until they had compelled me, on pain of attending his funeral, to purchase their tickets out of my father's estate.

Much more difficult, however, was the problem of my mother, who had thus unexpectedly survived her husband, and for whom I was therefore obliged, as I had promised my father, to make some sort of provision. This was the more harassing, too, in that my father's savings had been practically obliterated by his law costs, thereby reducing my own inheritance to the bare sum for which he had been insured. Further diminished by an iniquitous taxation, the settlement of bills, and the expenses of his interment, I was thus faced, in respect of my mother, with a singularly annoying predicament – and this at the very moment when my attention was fully occupied with the details of my wedding. Great was my satisfaction, therefore, when my fiancée, with an intelligence as welcome as it was unexpected, suggested that my mother should continue her previous functions in the house that we had procured at Stoke Newington. She would thus not only be assured of food and shelter, but would enjoy the additional satisfaction of enabling us to dispense, in our new home, with the paid services of a cook.

'A good idea,' I cried, 'an excellent idea,' and I remember Tact's pleasure when I gave her a kiss. So astounding, however, was my mother's reception of the plan that I was obliged to sit down for several minutes, while the scene recurred to me in the form of a nightmare on at least three occasions during the following fortnight.

'No,' said my mother. 'I'm very sorry, Augustus. But my future arrangements won't permit of it.'

I stared at her.

'Your future arrangements?' I said.

'Yes,' she replied. 'I'm going to take a holiday.'

It was then that I sat down.

'Take a holiday?' I asked.

'Yes, a holiday,' she said. 'Don't you think it's time?'

'But, my dear mother,' I said, 'what do you want a holiday for?'

'Why, just to see,' she replied, 'what it's like.'

I felt the blood rush to my cheeks.

'But, my dear mother,' I said, 'I can't consent to that.'

She folded her hands, not very agreeably.

'Then I'm afraid,' she said, 'that I shall have to go without.'

I looked at her.

'Go without?' I asked. 'But you can't. You haven't any money.'

She smiled a little.

'Oh, yes, I have,' she said. 'Quite sufficient for my purpose.'

I bent forward for a moment, struggling for breath.

'Sufficient for your purpose?' I asked. 'But where did you get it?'

'Oh, I've always saved a bit,' she said, 'and taken good advice, and I bought an annuity yesterday morning.'

'An annuity?' I repeated. 'You've saved enough for that?'

'Yes, and a little more,' she said, 'to play about with.'

'But, my dear mother,' I said, 'what did you save it out of?'

'Out of my housekeeping money,' she said. 'I made it rather a hobby.'

I rose to my feet again.

'Then what it amounts to,' I said, 'is that you've been robbing my poor father.'

'I think not,' she said, 'though you can consult Mr Balfour Whey, of course. But you must remember that I've had no wages.'

'Wages?' I cried. 'But you weren't a servant.'

'No, that's true,' she said. 'I was only a wife.'

'And a mother,' I reminded her. 'You seem to forget that.'

'Not at all,' she replied. 'I remember it distinctly.'

I looked at her sternly.

'Then am I to understand,' I asked, 'that you entirely refuse to accept my offer?'

'Yes, I'm afraid so,' she said. 'I'm going to Paris, and then to a little place on the Riviera.'

I resumed my seat rather heavily.

'To Paris?' I said. 'But you don't know the language.'

'*Pas trop*,' she said, '*mais ça suffit*. And besides, I shall be staying with Emily Smith.'

Totally unmanned, I wiped my forehead.

'But I thought she was in service,' I said, 'in Aberdeen.'

My mother smiled again.

'Oh, no,' she replied. 'She's running an hotel near Bordighera.'

Then, as the room rocked, I clutched at the arms of my chair.

'I'm feeling unwell,' I said. 'I'm going to be sick.'

'Yes, I was afraid,' said my mother, 'that you might be. You oughtn't to have eaten quite so much dinner.'

Thus with a heartlessness only the more incredible in view of the atmosphere with which she had been surrounded, my mother withdrew from her son's life, needless to say never to re-enter it; and we were consequently obliged to procure a professional cook at a not inconsiderable monthly wage.

Apart from this, however, after a satisfactory wedding service, adequately conducted by the Reverend Simeon Whey, the earlier years of my matrimonial life may be passed over without particular comment. Subject to my agreement with Ezekiel, who was now deteriorating almost every day, I had obtained, as I have said, a house at Stoke Newington, within easy distance of St Gregory's Church. Here, like my father, I soon made myself a sidesman, and within three or four months of joining the congregation, I had become the means of distributing the parish magazine in Longfellow Crescent and Byron Square. From that it was but a step to auditing the accounts of the Band of Hope and the Additional Blanket Fund, and in a very few years I was perhaps the most prominent figure in the parochial life of St Gregory's. Nor must it be supposed that I had entirely severed myself from all my previous regenerative interests. From the Anti-Dramatic and Saltatory Union it was true that I had deemed it better to resign, and indeed this body, lacking the support of Ezekiel, concluded its activities shortly afterwards. But I still retained my membership of the Non-Smokers' League, and for some years have been its deputy chairman, while I had had myself transferred, on moving to Stoke Newington, to the Dalston Division of the *S. P. S. D. T.*

Perhaps the happiest day, however, of this period of my life, and the one that finally led me to my present abode, was the October Saturday on which I heard from Simeon Whey that he had obtained the living of St Potamus, Hornsey. As this was only achieved after long years of practically ceaseless struggle, he wept in my arms, I remember, for nearly an hour, my wife and her sisters adding contributory tears.

'Nor will my happiness,' he said, 'be complete – kck –until I have seen the name of Augustus Carp publicly inscribed – kck – on the church notice board, as one of the churchwardens of my parish.'

Without delay, therefore, I resolved to transfer my worship to the church presided over by my friend, and within six months I had obtained the ten years' tenancy of Wilhelmina, Nassington Park Gardens. This I have since renewed, and as sidesman, churchwarden, Sunday School superintendent and secretary of the Glee Club, no less than as President of the St Potamus Purity League, I could scarcely have done otherwise. And indeed I rather fear that were I to suggest leaving, I should be forcibly prevented by my fellow-parishioners. My wife and her sisters, too, as they have frequently told me, have never regretted leaving Camberwell, slightly disturbed, as they have occasionally been, by the acute decline of their brother Ezekiel.

They have seldom seen him, however, and then but accidentally, and as for myself I have only met him once, when I chanced to encounter him at the entrance of the

Albany, where, as I understood, he then had chambers. Completely shaved and evidently massaged, he was flicking a particle of dust from his left coat-sleeve, and on catching sight of me, he surveyed me through a monocle with a thin gold chain and a tortoise-shell rim.

'Hullo, Carp,' he said. 'Taxi,' and a taxi being present, I was spared from replying.

Nor have I been denied – albeit it was not until a year ago that Providence saw fit to reward my efforts – the crowning satisfaction of becoming the father of a small, but still surviving, boy; and the happiest auguries, I think, can safely be discerned in the circumstances surrounding his birth. Indeed so amazingly similar were these to those ushering in my own that I cannot do better, perhaps, than close this volume with a scene from which my readers, I hope, will derive as intense a joy as that which was conferred upon myself.

Born at half-past three on a February morning, the world having been decked with a slight snowfall, it was then that the trained nurse in attendance on the case opened the bedroom door and emerged on the landing. I had gone outside to lean over the gate, and was still leaning there when she opened the door, but Faith and Hope, with Simeon Whey's housekeeper, were standing with bowed heads at the foot of the stairs. Prone in the parlour, and stretched in uneasy attitudes, Charity and Understanding were snatching a troubled sleep, while two female members of the St Potamus Purity League were upon their knees in the back kitchen. But for the fact indeed that Charity and Understanding had slight impediments in their noses, the whole house would have been wrapped in the profoundest stillness.

Simeon Whey's housekeeper was the first to see the nurse, though she only saw her, as it were, through a mist. The nurse was the first to speak in a voice tremulous with emotion.

'Where's Mr Carp?' she said.

'He's just gone outside,' said Simeon Whey's housekeeper.

Something splashed heavily on the hall linoleum. It was a drop of moisture from the nurse's forehead.

'Tell him,' she said, 'that he's the father of a son.'

Simeon Whey's housekeeper gave a great cry. I was beside her in a single leap. Always highly coloured, I have since been assured that my face seemed literally on fire. The two fellow-members of the St Potamus Purity League, accompanied by Charity and Understanding, rushed into the hall. The nurse leaned over the banisters.

'A boy,' she said. 'It's a boy.'

'A boy?' I said.

'Yes, a boy,' said the nurse.

There was a moment's hush, and then Nature had its way. Unashamedly I burst into tears. Simeon Whey's housekeeper kissed me on the neck just as the two fellow-members burst into a hymn; and a moment later, Charity and Understanding burst simultaneously into the doxology. Then I recovered myself and held up my hand.

'I shall call him Augustus,' I said, 'after myself.'

'Or tin?' suggested Simeon Whey's housekeeper. 'What about calling him tin, after the saint?'

'How do you mean tin?' I said.

'Augus-tin,' said Charity.

But I shook my head.

'No, it shall be tus,' I said. 'Tus is better than tin.'

Then Charity and Understanding resumed the singing, from which the two fellow-members had been unable to desist, until after rapidly thinking, and coming to a further decision, I once again held up my hand.

'And I shall give Simeon Whey,' I said, 'the first opportunity of becoming Augustus's godfather.'

Then I took a deep breath, threw back my shoulders, tilted my chin, and closed my eyes; and with the full vigour of my immense voice, I, too, joined in the doxology.